A Thousand Days for Mokhtar

BY PAUL BOWLES

A Thousand Days
for Mokhtar

and Other Stories

PAUL BOWLES

PETER OWEN · LONDON

ISBN 0 7206 07159

This collection first published in Great Britain 1989
© Paul Bowles 1944, 1945, 1946, 1947, 1948, 1949,
1952, 1957, 1984, 1985

Peter Owen Ltd gratefully acknowledge permission from Tombouctou
Press, San Francisco, for permission to reprint the stories 'Unwelcome
Words' and 'Julian Vreden', and Black Sparrow Press for permission to
reprint all the other stories in this volume.

PETER OWEN PUBLISHERS
73 Kenway Road London SW5 0RE

Photoset by Bookworm Typesetting, Manchester
Printed in Great Britain by Billings of Worcester

Preface

As we know, creativity is an eruption of the unconscious. Exposed to the light of reason, this subterranean material generally discovers the uses to which it will be put, and the form it will assume. The author, aware of what he is doing, gives it an argument and a voice. The end product is man-made. Most of the tales in this collection adhere to this formula.

There is, however, another way of treating this basic material, which is to use it 'raw', without questioning its sense, allowing it to cool and harden into its own natural shape. Here the author remains ignorant of what he has written, and is not likely to be able to assign a 'meaning' to it, inasmuch as that consideration did not occur to him during its composition. Two of the present stories were written thus: *The Scorpion* and *By the Water*. Another, *Tapiama*, owes its lack of form and consistent meaning to a different circumstance: a protracted high fever which kept me on the brink of delirium for several days before I was hospitalized.

A fourth story, *You Are Not I*, although consciously shaped after the first page, had a more unusual birth. I dreamed I was looking at a printed page. As I read it, I knew it was by me, while at the same time I was aware that I had not yet written it. I read it carefully, reread it, and woke up. Then in the darkness I reached for the notebook and pencil I kept beside my bed and scribbled, still in the dark, the text as far as I had memorized it. The next morning, keeping the dreamed sentences just as I'd notated them, and using them as the opening of the piece, I continued to write. I was not surprised when the tale, as a result of my insistence upon incorporating the dreamed material word for word, turned out to be the work of a psychopath.

Paul Bowles

Contents

How Many Midnights

How many midnights, she wondered, had she raised the shade, opened the big window, and leaned out to gaze across the gently stirring city towards the highest towers? Over there behind a certain unmistakable group of them was his building, and at the very top of the building was his apartment, six flights up. In the summer she would look out over the roof-tops at some length and sigh, and during the hottest weeks she moved her bed over, directly under the window. Then she would turn off all the lights and sit on the bed combing her hair in the glowing dimness of the city night, or sometimes even by moonlight, which of course was perfect. In the winter, however, she had to content herself with a moment of looking and a flash of imagining before she bounded across the room into bed.

It was winter now. She was walking crosstown, east, along one of the late Forties. This part of town always had seemed vaguely mysterious to her because of its specially constructed buildings that did not quite touch the pavement. All the buildings just north of the Grand Central were built that way, to absorb the shock, Van had told her; and there were long stretches of grillework in the sidewalks through which, particularly at night, one could see another world beneath: railway tracks and sometimes a slowly moving train. When it snowed, as it was doing now, the snow filtered down through the grilles and covered the ties; then they were even more apparent.

Van worked here in this neighbourhood: he was manager of a large bookshop and lending library on Madison Avenue. And he lived in the neighbourhood as well, only further over

9

east, between Third and Second Avenues. His place was not ideal, either as to actual physical comfort or as to locality (since the immediate district was clearly a slum), but with her help he had made it liveable, and she used to tell him: 'New York and Paris, are like that: no clear demarcation of neighbourhoods.'

In any case, they already had signed a sub-lease for a place near Gramercy Park which was to be free the first of March. This was of prime importance because they planned to marry on Valentine's Day. They were by no means sentimental souls, either one of them, and for that very reason it seemed to June a little daring to announce to their friends during cocktails: 'It's to be Valentine's Day.'

Her father, who always was to be counted on to do the thoughtful thing, was staking them to two weeks in Bermuda. 'God knows why,' Van said. 'He hates my guts.'

'I don't know how you can say a thing like that about Dad,' objected June. 'He's never been anything but the essence of politeness with you.'

'That's right,' said Van, but impenitently.

She crossed Lexington Avenue. The entire sky looked as though it were being illumined from above by grey-violet neons. The tops of the buildings were lost in the cloud made by the falling snow. And the harbour sounds, instead of coming from the river ahead, came from above, as if the tugs were making their careful way around the tips of the towers. This is the way New York was meant to be, she thought – not the crowded fire-escape, open-hydrant, sumac-leaved summer. Just this quiet, damp, neutral weather when the water seemed all around. She stood still a moment in the middle of the block, listening to the foghorns; there was a whole perspective of them. In the remotest background was a very faint, smothered one that said: 'Mmmmm! Mmmmm!' It must be on the Sound, she thought. She started to walk again.

In her coat-pocket she had the keys, because this was to be a special night. Not that there had been any overt reference to that: there was no need for it. It had been implicit in their conversation yesterday afternoon when she had stopped in at the bookshop to see him. They had stood a few minutes talking in the back of the store among the desks, and then he had slipped her the keys. That was surely the most exciting single thing that ever had happened between them – the passage of the keys from his hand to hers. By the gesture he gave up what she knew was most dear to him: his privacy. She did not want him to think that she was in any way unaware of this, and she said in a low voice: 'You can trust me with them, I think,' laughing immediately afterwards so that her remark should not sound ridiculous. He had kissed her and they had gone out for ten minutes to have coffee.

Sitting at the counter he had told how he had caught a man stealing books the night before. (The bookshop was open at night; because of the location it seemed they did almost as much business in the evening as they did during the day.) Van had just finished arranging a display of new books in one of the show windows, and was standing outside in the street looking in. He had noticed a man wearing a long overcoat, standing by the technical books. 'I had my eye on him from the beginning. It's a type, you know. You get to spot them. He looked at me right through the window. I suppose he thought I was just another man in the street. I had on *my* overcoat, too.' And the man had taken a quick glance around the store to be sure that no one was watching him, had reached up, snatched down a book and dropped it inside his coat. Van had gone quickly to the corner, tapped the traffic policeman on the shoulder and said: 'Would you mind coming into my store for a minute? I want you to arrest a man.' They had caught him, and when they had opened his coat they found he already had taken three books.

Van always said: 'You see some funny things in a bookshop', and often they were really funny. But this story struck June as remotely sinister rather than amusing. Not because it had to do with a theft, certainly. It was not the first case of book lifting he had related to her. Perhaps it was because more than anything else she hated being watched behind her back, and involuntarily she put herself in the place of the thief, with whom she felt that Van had not been quite fair. It seemed to her that he might have gone in and said to him: 'I've been watching you. I've seen everything you've been doing. Now, I give you one last chance. Put back whatever you've taken and get the hell out, and don't come back in here.' To spring on the man out of the dark after spying on him did seem a little unfair. But she knew she was being absurd. Van could never be unfair with anyone; this was his way of handling the affair, and it was typical of him: he never would argue. She never knew even when he was angry with her until after it was all over, and he told her, smiling: 'Gee, I was burned up last Friday.'

She crossed Third Avenue. Up to now the snow had been melting as fast as it fell, but the air was getting colder, and the sidewalk began to show silver. The keys jingled in her coat pocket; she pulled off her glove and felt for them. They also were cold. When she had left her house, she had said to her parents: 'I'm going out with Van. I'll probably be rather late.' They had merely said: 'Yes.' But she thought she had intercepted a look of mutual understanding between them. It was all right: in ten more days they would be married. She had climbed up the six steep flights of stairs on a good many evenings during the past two years, just to spend an hour or so with him, but never, she reflected with an obscure sort of pride, had anything ever occurred between them which was not what her parents would call 'honourable'.

She had arrived at the apartment house; it had a grey-stone façade and a good deal of wrought iron around the entrance door. A woman who looked like a West Indian of some sort came out. Noticing that June was carrying a potted plant under her arm, she held the door partially open for her. June thanked her and went in. It was a rubber plant she had bought for Van's apartment. He was inclined to be indifferent about flowers, and, she feared, about decoration in general. She always had hoped to develop aesthetic appreciation in him, and she considered that she had made remarkable progress during the past year. Practically all the adornments in his apartment were objects either of her buying or her choosing.

She knew just how many steps there were to each flight of stairs: nineteen for the first and fifteen for the others. The halls were tiled in black and white, like a bathroom, and tonight, to add to that impression, the stairs and floors were thoroughly wet with the melting snow people had tracked in;

the air smelled of wet doormats, wet rubbers, wet clothing. On the third floor a huge perambulator of black leatherette nearly blocked the passageway between the stairs. She frowned at it and thought of the fire regulations.

Because she did not want to be out of breath she mounted the stairs slowly. Not that Van would be there when she arrived – it was still too early – but being out of breath always created in her a false kind of excitement which she particularly wanted to avoid tonight. She turned the key in the lock and stepped inside. It gave her a strange sensation to push open the door all by herself and stand there in the hall alone, smelling the special odour of the place: an amalgam in which she imagined she detected furniture polish, shaving-cream and wood-smoke. Wood-smoke there surely was, because he had a fireplace. It was she who had persuaded him to have it installed. And it had not been nearly so expensive to build as he had imagined it was going to be, because since this was the top floor the chimney had only to be built up through the roof. Many times he had said to her: 'That was one sensible idea you had', as though the others had not been just as good! They had cut down the legs of all the living-room furniture so that it nestled nearer the floor and made the room seem spacious; they had painted each wall a different shade of grey, adding the occasional wall brackets of ivy; they had bought the big glass coffee-table. All these things had made the place pleasanter, and they had all been her ideas.

She shut the door and went into the kitchen. It was a little chilly in the apartment; she lit the gas oven. Then she unwrapped the wet brown paper from around the rubber plant, and set the pot upright on the table. The plant leaned somewhat to one side. She tried to make it stand straight, but it would not. The ice-box motor was purring. She took out two trays of ice and dumped the cubes into a bowl. Reaching up to the top shelf of the cabinet she brought down an almost full bottle of Johnny Walker, and set it, along with two highball glasses, on to the big lacquer tray. The room suddenly seemed terribly close; she turned off the oven. Then she scurried about looking for newspapers with which to lay a fire. There were only a few, but she found some old magazines in the kitchen. She rolled the newspapers into thin little logs and set them at various angles across the andirons. Underneath she pushed crumpled pages of the magazines, and on top she put what kindling wood there was. The logs she decided to leave until the kindling already was burning. When the fire was laid, but not lighted, she looked out of the window. The snow was coming down thicker than it had been when she came in. She drew the heavy woollen curtains; they covered one entire wall, and they too had been her idea. Van had wanted to have venetian blinds made. She had tried to make him see how hideous they would be, but although he had agreed that the black-and-white curtains were smart, he never would admit that venetian blinds were ugly. 'Maybe you're right, for this room,' he said. 'For every room in the world,' she had wanted to declare, but she decided against it, since after all he had given in.

It wasn't that Van had really bad taste. He had an innate sensitivity and a true intelligence which became manifest whenever he talked about the books he had read (and he read a good many during odd moments at the bookshop). But his aesthetic sense had never been fully awakened. Naturally she never mentioned it – she merely made small suggestions which he was free to take or to leave as he saw fit. And usually, if she let her little hints fall at strategic moments, he would take them.

On the mantel were two enormous plaster candelabra covered with angels; she had brought them herself all the way from Matamoros Izúcar in Mexico. Actually she had packed six of them, and all had broken except these two which did not quite match, one of them being somewhat taller than the other. (These were among the few things about which Van was still a bit recalcitrant: he could not be sure he liked them, even yet.) Each one held six candles. She went to a drawer in the desk and got out a dozen long yellow tapers. Often she brought him a dozen at a time. 'Where am I supposed to put the damned things?' he would complain. She got a knife from the kitchen and began to scrape the bottoms of the candles to make them fit the holders. In the middle of this operation he's going to arrive, she said to herself. She wanted the place to be perfect before he got there. Nervously she tossed the paraffin scrapings into the fireplace. She had a feeling that he would not just come up; it would be more like him to ring from the vestibule downstairs. At least, she hoped he would do that. The time it would take him to get up the six flights might make a great difference in the way the room would look. She fitted the last candle into the bright holder and sighed with relief. They were slow-burning ones; she decided to light them now before returning the candelabra to the mantel. Up there they looked beautiful. She stepped back to admire their splendour, and for a moment watched the slowly moving interplay of shadows on the wall. She switched off the electric lights in the room. With the fireplace aglow the effect would be breathtaking.

Impetuously she determined to do a very daring thing. It might possibly annoy Van when he first saw it, but she would do it anyway. She rushed to the other side of the room and feverishly began to push the divan across the floor towards the fireplace. It would be so snug to be right in front of the blaze, especially with the snow outside. The cushions fell off and a castor got entangled with the long wool of the goatskin rug she had given him for his birthday. She got the rug out of the way and continued to manipulate the divan. It looked absurd out there in the middle of the room, and she swung one end around so that it lay at right angles to the fireplace, against the wall. After she had piled the cushions back she stepped aside to observe it, and decided to leave it there. Then the other pieces had to be arranged. The whole room was in disorder at this point.

I know he's going to open that door this minute, she thought. She turned the overhead light on and quickly began to shift chairs, lamps and tables. The last piece to be moved was a small commode that she had once helped him sandpaper. As she carried it across the room its one little drawer slid out and fell on the floor. All the letters Van had received in the past months were there, lying in a fairly compact heap at her feet. 'Damnation!' she said aloud, and as she said it, the hideous metallic sound of the buzzer in the kitchen echoed through the apartment. She let go of the commode and rushed out to press the button that opened the door downstairs on to the street. Then, without pressing it, she ran back into the living-room and knelt on the floor, quickly gathering up the letters and dumping them into the drawer. But they had been piled carefully into that small space before the accident, and now they were not; as a result the drawer was over-full and would not close. Again she spoke aloud. 'Oh, my God!' she said. And she said that because for no reason at all it had occurred to her that Van might think she had been reading all his correspondence. The main thing now was to get the commode over into the corner; then she might be able to force the drawer shut. As she lifted it, the buzzer pealed again, with insistence. She ran into the kitchen, and this time pressed the answer button with all her might. Swiftly she hurried back and carried the commode into the corner. Then she tried to close the drawer and found it an impossibility. In a burst of inspiration she turned the little piece of furniture around so that the drawer opened towards the wall. She stepped to the fireplace and touched a match to the paper logs. By now he would have got only about to the fourth floor; there were three more.

She turned off the light once again, went into the hall and looked at herself briefly in the mirror, put out the light there, and moved towards the entrance door. With her hand on the knob, she held her breath, and found that her heart was beating much too fast. It was just what she had not wanted. She had hoped to have him step into a little world of absolute calm. And now because of that absurd drawer she was upset. Or perhaps it was the dragging around of all that furniture. She opened the door a crack and listened. A second later she stepped out into the hall, and again she listened. She walked to the stairs. 'Van?' she called, and immediately she was furious with herself.

A man's voice answered from two floors below. 'Riley?' he yelled.

'What?' she cried.

'I'm looking for Riley.'

'You've rung the wrong bell,' she shouted, enunciating the words very distinctly in spite of her raised voice.

She went in and shut the door, holding on to the knob and leaning her forehead against the panel for a moment. Now her heart was beating even more violently. She returned to the commode in the corner. I might as well fix it once and for all right now, she thought. Otherwise her mind would be on it every instant. She turned it around, took out all the letters and carefully replaced them in four equal piles. Even then the drawer shut with difficulty, but it did close. When that was done, she went to the window and pulled back the curtain. It seemed to be growing much colder. The wind had risen; it was blowing from the east. The sky was no longer violet. It was black. She could see the snow swirling past the street lamp below. She wondered if it were going to turn into a blizzard. Tomorrow was Sunday; she simply would stay on. There would be a terrible moment in the morning, of course, when her parents arose and found she had not come in, but she would not be there to see it, and she could make it up with them later. And what an ideal little vacation it would make: a night and day up there in the snow, isolated from everything, shut away from everyone but Van. As she watched the street, she gradually became convinced that the storm would last all night. She looked back into the room. It gave her keen pleasure to contrast its glow with the hostile night outside. She let the curtain fall and went to the fireplace. The kindling was at the height of its blazing and there was no more; she piled two small logs on top of it. Soon they were crackling with such energy that she thought it wise to put the screen across in front of them. She sat on the divan looking at her legs in the blended fire-light and candle-glow. Smiling, she leaned back against the cushions. Her heart was no longer racing. She felt almost calm. The wind whined outside; to her it was inevitably a melancholy sound. Even tonight.

Suddenly she decided that it would be inexcusable not to let her parents know she was staying the night. She went into the bedroom and lay on the bed, resting the telephone on her stomach. It moved ridiculously while she dialled. Her mother, not her father, answered. Thank God, she said to herself, and she let her head fall back upon the pillows. Her mother had been asleep; she did not sound too pleased to have been called to the telephone. 'You're all right, I hope,' she said. They spoke of the storm. 'Yes, it's awful out,' said June. 'Oh, no, I'm at Van's. We have a fire. I'm going to stay. All night.' There was a short silence. 'Well, I think you're very foolish,' she heard her mother say. And she went on. June let her talk a bit. Then she interrupted, letting a note of impatience sound in her voice. 'I can't very well discuss it now. You understand.' Her mother's voice was shrill. 'No, I *don't* understand!' she cried. She was taking it more seriously than June had expected. 'I can't talk now,' said June. 'I'll see you tomorrow.' She said good-night and hung up, lying perfectly still for a moment. Then she lifted the telephone and set it on the night table, but still she did not move. When she had heard herself say: 'We have a fire,' a feeling of dread had seized her. It was as if in giving voice to the pretence she thereby became conscious of it. Van had not yet arrived; why then had she taken care to speak as though he had? She could only have been trying to reassure herself. Again her heart had begun to beat heavily. And finally she did what she had been trying not even to think of doing ever since she had arrived: she looked at her watch.

It was a little after midnight. There was absolutely no doubt about it; already he was quite late. He no longer could arrive without going into explanations. Something must have happened, and it only could be something bad. 'Ridiculous!' she cried in anger, jumping up and going out into the kitchen. The ice cubes had melted a good deal; she poured the cold water into the sink between her spread fingers, and shook the cubes around in the bowl petulantly, trying to stem the resentment she felt rising up inside her. It will be interesting to know what his excuse will be, she said to herself. She decided that when he arrived her only possible behaviour would be to pretend not to have noticed his lateness.

She dropped some of the ice cubes into one of the glasses, poured in some Scotch, stirred it, and went into the living-room with it. The fire was burning triumphantly; the whole room danced in flamelight. She sat on the couch and downed her drink, a little too quickly for a young woman completely at her ease, which was what she was trying to be. When she had finished the last drop, she forced herself to sit without moving for ten minutes by her watch. Then she went out and made herself another drink, a little stronger.

This one she drank walking thoughtfully around and around the centre of the room. She was fighting against an absurd impulse to put on her coat and go into the street to look for him. Old woman, she said to herself. Old people always had that reaction – they always expected tragedies. As she came to the end of her second drink she succeeded in convincing herself that the mathematical probabilities of Van's having met with his first serious accident on this particular evening were extremely slight. This moral certitude engendered a feeling of light-heartedness, which expressed itself in the desire for a third drink. She had only just begun this one when an even sharper anguish seized her. If it was not likely that he had had an accident, it was utterly unthinkable that he should have let some unforeseen work detain him until this late; he would have telephoned her anyway. It was even more inconceivable that their rendezvous should have slipped his mind. The final, remaining possibility therefore was that he had deliberately avoided it, which of course was absurd. She tossed another log on to the fire. Again she went to the window and peered between the curtains down into the empty street. The wind had become a gale. She felt each blast against her face through the closed window. Listening for sounds of traffic, she heard none; even the boats seemed to have been silenced. Only the rushing of the wind was left – that and the occasional faint hissing of the fine snow against the glass. She burst into tears; she did not know whether it was out of self-pity, anger and humiliation, loneliness, or just plain nervousness.

As she stood there in the window with the tears covering her sight, it occurred to her how ironic it would be if he should come and find her like this: slightly drunk, sobbing, with her make-up surely in a state of a complete ruin. A sound behind her ended her weeping instantly. She let go of the curtain and turned to face the room: through her tears she could see nothing but quivering webs of light. She squeezed her lids tightly together: one of the logs had broken in two. The smaller half lay on the hearth smoking. She went over and kicked it into the fire. Then she tiptoed into the hall to the entrance door and slipped the chain on. As soon as she had done that she was terrified. It was nothing less than a symbol of fear – she realized it as she looked at the brass links stretching across from jamb to door. But once having put it up, she did not have the courage to take it down again.

Still on tiptoe, she returned to the living-room and lay on the divan, burying her face in the cushions. She was not crying any longer – she felt too empty and frightened to do anything but lie quite still. But after a while she sat up and looked slowly about the room. The candles had burned down half-way; she looked at them, at the ivy trailing down from the little pots on the wall, at the white goatskin by her feet, at the striped curtains. They were all hers. 'Van, Van,' she said under her breath. Unsteadily she rose and made her way to the bathroom. The glaring light hurt her eyes. Hanging on the inside of the door was Van's old flannel bathrobe. It was too big for her, but she got into it and rolled the sleeves back, turning up the collar and pulling the belt tightly about her waist. In the living-room she lay down again on the divan among the cushions. From time to time she rubbed her cheek against the wool of the sleeve under her face. She stared into the fire.

Van was in the room. It was daylight out – a strange grey dawn. She sat up, feeling light-headed. 'Van,' she said. He was moving slowly across the floor towards the window. And the curtains had been drawn back. There was the rectangle of dim white sky, with Van going towards it. She called to him again. If he heard her he paid no attention. She sat back, watching. Now and then he shook his head slowly from side to side; the gesture made her feel like crying again, but not for herself this time. It was quite natural that he should be there, shuffling slowly across the room in the pale early light, shaking his head from one side to the other. Suddenly she said to herself that he was looking for something, that he might find it, and she began to shiver sitting up there in the cold. He has found it, she thought, but he's pretending he hasn't because he knows I'm watching him. And even as the idea formed itself in her mind she saw him reach up and swing himself through the window. She screamed, jumped down from the couch and ran across the room. When she got to the window there was nothing to see but the vast grey panorama of a city at dawn, spitefully clear in every tiniest detail. She stood there looking out, a hundred storeys above the ground, seeing for miles up and down the empty streets. It was a foreign city. And in her sleep she was able somehow to know she was sleeping, and to efface the scene.

The sputtering of a candle as it went out roused her. Several of them had already burned out. The shadows on the ceiling were wavering like bats. The room was cold and the curtains across the closed window moved inward with the force of the wind. She lay perfectly still. In the fireplace she heard the powdery, faintly metallic sound of a cooling ember as it fell. For a long time she remained unmoving. Then she sprang up, turned on all the lights, went into the bedroom and stood for a moment looking at the telephone. The sight of it calmed her a little. She took off the bathrobe and opened the closet door to hang it up. She knew his luggage by heart; his small overnight valise was missing. Slowly her mouth opened. She did not think to put her hand over it.

She slipped on her coat and unhooked the chain on the entrance door. The hall outside was full of scurrying draughts. Down the six flights she ran, one after the other, until she was at the front door. The snow had drifted high, completely covering the steps. She went out. It was bitter cold in the wind, but only a stray flake fell now and then. She stood there. The street did not tell her what to do. She began to wade through the deep snow, eastward. A taxi, moving cautiously down Second Avenue, its chains clanking rhythmically, met her at the corner. She hailed it, got in.

'Take me to the river,' she said, pointing.

'What street?'

'Any street that goes down all the way.'

Almost immediately they were there. She got out, paid the driver, walked slowly to the end of the pavement, and stood watching. The dawn was really breaking now, but it was very different from the one she had seen through the window. The wind took her breath away, the water out there was alive. Against the winter sky across the river there were factories. The lights of a small craft moved further down in midstream. She clenched her fists. A terrible anguish had taken possession of her. She was trembling, but she did not feel the cold. Abruptly she turned around. The driver was standing in the street blowing into his cupped hands. And he was looking at her intently.

'You're not waiting for me, are you?' she said. (Was that her voice?)

'Yes, *ma'am,'* he said with force.

'I didn't tell you to.' (With her whole life falling to pieces before her, how was it that her voice rang with such asperity, such hard self-assurance?)

'That's right.' He put his gloves back on. 'Take your time,' he said.

She turned her back on him and watched the changing water. Suddenly she felt ridiculous. She went over to the cab, got in, and gave her home address.

The doorman was asleep when she rang, and even after she was inside she had to wait nearly five minutes for the elevator boy to bring the car up from the basement. She tiptoed through the apartment to her room, shutting the door behind her. When she had undressed she opened the big window without looking out, and got into bed. The cold wind blew through the room.

You Are Not I

You are not I. No one but me could possibly be. I know that, and I know where I have been and what I have done ever since yesterday when I walked out the gate during the train wreck. Everyone was so excited that no one noticed me. I became completely unimportant as soon as it was a question of cut people and smashed cars down there on the tracks. We girls all went running down the bank when we heard the noise, and we landed against the cyclone fence like a lot of monkeys. Mrs Werth was chewing on her crucifix and crying her eyes out. I suppose it hurt her lips. Or maybe she thought one of her daughters was on the train down there. It was really a bad accident; anyone could see that. The spring rains had dissolved the earth that kept the ties firm, and so the rails had spread a little and the train had gone into the ditch. But how everyone could get so excited I still fail to understand.

I always hated the trains, hated to see them go by down there, hated to see them disappear way off up the valley toward the next town. It made me angry to think of all those people moving from one town to another, without any right to. Whoever said to them: 'You may go and buy your ticket and make the trip this morning to Reading. You will go past twenty-three stations, over forty bridges, through three tunnels, and still keep going, if you want to, even after you get to Reading'? No one. I know that. I know there is no chief who says things like that to people. But it makes it pleasanter for me when I imagine such a person does exist. Perhaps it would be only a tremendous voice speaking over a public-address system set up in all the main streets.

23

When I saw the train down there helpless on its side like an old worm knocked off a plant, I began to laugh. But I held on to the fence very hard when the people started to climb out the windows bleeding.

I was up in the courtyard, and there was the paper wrapper off a box of Cheese Tid Bits lying on the bench. Then I was at the main gate, and it was open. A black car was outside at the kerb, and a man was sitting in front smoking. I thought of speaking to him and asking him if he knew who I was, but I decided not to. It was a sunny morning full of sweet air and birds. I followed the road around the hill, down to the tracks. Then I walked up the tracks feeling excited. The dining car looked strange lying on its side with the window glass all broken and some of the cloth shades drawn down. A robin kept whistling in a tree above. Of course, I said to myself. This is just in man's world. If something real should happen, they would stop singing. I walked up and down along the cinder bed beside the track, looking at the people lying in the bushes. Men were beginning to carry them up toward the front end of the train where the road crosses the tracks. There was a woman in a white uniform, and I tried to keep from passing close to her.

I decided to go down a wide path that led through the blackberry bushes, and in a small clearing I found an old stove with a lot of dirty bandages and handkerchiefs in the rubbish around the base of it. Underneath everything was a pile of stones. I found several round ones and some others. The earth here was very soft and moist. When I got back to the train there seemed to be a lot more people running around. I walked close to the ones who were lying side by side on the cinders, and looked at their faces. One was a girl and her mouth was open. I dropped one of the stones in and went on. A fat man also had his mouth open. I put in a sharp stone that looked like a piece of coal. It occurred to me that I might not have enough stones for them all, and the cinders were too small. There was one old woman walking up and down wiping her hands on her skirt very quickly, over and over again. She had on a long black silk dress with a design of blue mouths stamped all over it. Perhaps they were supposed to be leaves but they were formed like mouths. She looked crazy to me and I kept clear of her. Suddenly I noticed a hand with rings on the fingers sticking out from under a lot of bent pieces of metal. I tugged at the metal and saw a face. It was a woman and her mouth was closed. I tried to open it so I could get a stone in. A man grabbed me by the shoulder and pulled at me. He looked angry. 'What are you doing?' he yelled. 'Are you crazy?' I began to cry and said she was my sister. She did look a little like her, and I sobbed and kept saying: 'She's dead. She's dead.' The man stopped looking so angry and pushed me along toward the head of the train, holding my arm tightly with one hand. I tried to jerk away from him. At the same time I decided not to say anything more except 'She's dead' once in a while. 'That's all right,' the man said. When we got to the front end of the train he made me sit down on the grass embankment alongside a lot of other people. Some of them were crying, so I stopped and watched them.

It seemed to me that life outside was like life inside. There was always somebody to stop people from doing what they wanted to do. I smiled when I thought that this was just the opposite of what I had felt when I was still inside. Perhaps what we want to do is wrong, but why should they always be the ones to decide? I began to consider this as I sat there pulling the little new blades of grass out of the ground. And I thought that for once *I* would decide what was right, and do it.

It was not very long before several ambulances drove up. They were for us, the row of people sitting on the bank, as well as for the ones lying around on stretchers and overcoats. I don't know why, since the people weren't in pain. Or perhaps they were. When a great many people are in pain together they aren't so likely to make a noise about it, probably because no one listens. Of course I was in no pain at all. I could have told anyone that if I had been asked. But no one asked me. What they did ask me was my address, and I gave my sister's address because it is only a half-hour's drive. Besides, I stayed with her for quite a while before I went away, but that was years ago, I think. We all drove off together, some lying down inside the ambulances, and the rest of us sitting on an uncomfortable bench in one that had no bed. The woman next to me must have been a foreigner; she was moaning like a baby, and there was not a drop of blood on her that I could see, anywhere. I looked her all over very carefully on the way, but she seemed to resent it, and turned her face the other way, still crying. When we got to the hospital we were all taken in and examined. About me they just said: 'Shock,' and asked me again where I lived. I gave them the same address as before, and soon they took me out again and put me into the front seat of a sort of station-wagon, between the driver and another man, an attendant, I suppose. They both spoke to me about the weather, but I knew enough not to let myself be trapped that easily. I know how the simplest subject can suddenly twist around and choke you when you think you're quite safe. 'She's dead,' I said once, when we were half-way between the two towns. 'Maybe not, maybe not,' said the driver, as if he were talking to a child. I kept my head down most of the time, but I managed to count the gas stations as we went along.

When we arrived at my sister's house the driver got out and rang the bell. I had forgotten that the street was so ugly. The houses were built one against the other, all alike, with only a narrow cement walk between. And each one was a few feet lower than the other, so that the long row of them looked like an enormous flight of stairs. The children were evidently allowed to run wild over all the front yards, and there was no grass anywhere in sight, only mud.

My sister came to the door. The driver and she spoke a few words, and then I saw her look very worried very suddenly. She came out to the car and leaned in. She had new glasses, thicker than the others. She did not seem to be looking at me. Instead she said to the driver: 'Are you *sure* she's all right?'

'Absolutely,' he answered. 'I wouldn't be telling you if she wasn't. She's just been examined all over up at the hospital. It's just shock. A good rest will fix her up fine.' The attendant got out, to help me out and up the steps, although I could have gone perfectly well by myself. I saw my sister looking at me out of the corner of her eye the same as she used to. When I was on the porch I heard her whisper to the attendant: 'She don't look well yet to *me*.' He patted her arm and said: 'She'll be fine. Just don't let her get excited.'

'That's what they always said,' she complained, 'but she just *does*.'

The attendant got into the car. 'She ain't hurt at *all*, lady.' He slammed the door.

'Hurt!' exclaimed my sister, watching the car. It drove off and she stood following it with her eyes until it got to the top of the hill and turned. I was still looking down at the porch floor because I wasn't sure yet what was going to happen. I often feel that something is about to happen, and when I do, I stay perfectly still and let it go ahead. There's no use wondering about it or trying to stop it. At this time I had no particular feeling that a special event was about to come out, but I did feel that I would be more likely to do the right thing if I waited and let my sister act first. She stood where she was, in her apron, breaking off the tips of the pussywillow stems that stuck out of the bush beside her. She still refused to look at me. Finally she grunted: 'Might as well go on inside. It's cold out here.' I opened the door and walked in.

Right away I saw she had had the whole thing rebuilt, only backward. There was always a hall and a living-room, except that the hall used to be on the left-hand side of the living-room and now it was on the right. That made me wonder why I had failed to notice that the front door was now at the right end of the porch. She had even switched the stairs and fireplace around into each other's places. The furniture was the same, but each piece had been put into the position exactly opposite to the way it had been before. I decided to say nothing and let her do the explaining if she felt like it. It occurred to me that it must have cost her every cent she had in the bank, and still it looked exactly the same as it had when she began. I kept my mouth shut, but I could not help looking around with a good deal of curiosity to see if she had carried out the reversal in every detail.

I went into the living-room. The three big chairs around the centre table were still wrapped in old sheets, and the floor lamp by the pianola had the same torn cellophane cover on its shade. I began to laugh, everything looked so comical backward. I saw her grab the fringe of the portière and look at me hard. I went on laughing.

The radio next door was playing an organ selection. Suddenly my sister said: 'Sit down, Ethel. I've got something to do. I'll be right back.' She went into the kitchen through the hall and I heard the back door open.

I knew already where she was going. She was afraid of me, and she wanted Mrs Jelinek to come over. Sure enough, in a minute they both came in, and my sister walked right into the living-room this time. She looked angry now, but she had nothing to say. Mrs Jelinek is sloppy and fat. She shook hands with me and said: 'Well, well, old-timer!' I decided not to talk to her either because I distrust her, so I turned around and lifted the lid of the pianola. I tried to push down some keys, but the catch was on and they were all stiff and wouldn't move. I closed the lid and went over to see out the window. A little girl was wheeling a doll carriage along the sidewalk down the hill; she kept looking back at the tracks the wheels made when they left a wet part of the pavement and went on to a dry patch. I was determined not to let Mrs Jelinek gain any advantage over me, so I kept quiet. I sat down in the rocker by the window and began to hum.

Before long they started to talk to each other in low voices, but of course I heard everything they said. Mrs Jelinek said: 'I thought they was keeping her.' My sister said: 'I don't know. So did I. But the man kept telling me she was all right. Huh! She's just the same.' 'Why, sure,' said Mrs Jelinek. They were quiet a minute.

'Well, I'm not going to put up with it!' said my sister suddenly. 'I'm going to tell Dr Dunn what I think of him.'

'Call the Home,' urged Mrs Jelinek.

'I certainly am,' my sister answered. 'You stay here. I'll see if Kate's in.' She meant Mrs Schultz, who lives on the other side and has a telephone. I did not even look up when she went out. I had made a big decision, and that was to stay right in the house and under no condition let myself be taken back there. I knew it would be difficult, but I had a plan I knew would work if I used all my will-power. I have great will-power.

The first important thing to do was to go on keeping quiet, not to speak a word that might break the spell I was starting to work. I knew I would have to concentrate deeply, but that is easy for me. I knew it was going to be a battle between my sister and me, but I was confident that my force of character and superior education had fitted me for just such a battle, and that I could win it. All I had to do was to keep insisting inside myself, and things would happen the way I willed it. I said this to myself as I rocked. Mrs Jelinek stood in the hall doorway with her arms folded, mostly looking out the front door. By now life seemed much clearer and more purposeful than it had in a long, long time. This way I would have what I wanted. 'No one can stop you,' I thought.

It was a quarter of an hour before my sister came back. When she walked in she had both Mrs Schultz and Mrs Schultz's brother with her, and all three of them looked a little frightened. I knew exactly what had happened even before she told Mrs Jelinek. She had called the Home and complained to Dr Dunn that I had been released, and he had been very much excited and told her to hold on to me by all means because I had not been discharged at all but had somehow *got out*. I was a little shocked to hear it put that way, but now that I thought of it, I had to admit to myself that that was just what I had done.

I got up when Mrs Schultz's brother came in, and glared at him hard.

'Take it easy, now, Miss Ethel,' he said, and his voice sounded nervous. I bowed low to him: at least he was polite.

''Lo, Steve,' said Mrs Jelinek.

I watched every move they made. I would have died rather than let the spell be broken. I felt I could hold it together only by a great effort. Mrs Schultz's brother was scratching the side of his nose, and his other hand twitched in his pants pocket. I knew he would give me no trouble. Mrs Schultz and Mrs Jelinek would not go any further than my sister told them to. And she herself was terrified of me, for although I had never done her any harm, she had always been convinced that some day I would. It may be that she knew now what I was about to do to her, but I doubt it, or she would have run away from the house.

'When they coming?' asked Mrs Jelinek.

'Soon's they can get here,' said Mrs Schultz.

They all stood in the doorway.

'I see they rescued the flood victims, you remember last night on the radio?' said Mrs Schultz's brother.

Nobody answered. I was concentrating on my plan, and it took all my strength, so I sat down again.

'She'll be all right,' said Mrs Schultz's brother. He lit a cigarette and leaned back against the banisters.

The house was very ugly, but I already was getting ideas for making it look better. I have excellent taste in decoration. I tried not to think of those things, and said over and over inside my head: 'Make it work.'

Mrs Jelinek finally sat down on the couch by the door, pulled her skirts around her legs and coughed. She still looked red in the face and serious. I could have laughed out loud when I thought of what they were really waiting to see if they had only known it.

I heard a car door slam outside. I looked out. Two of the men from the Home were coming up the walk. Somebody else was sitting at the wheel, waiting. My sister went quickly to the front door and opened it. One of the men said: 'Where is she?' They both came in and stood a second looking at me and grinning.

'Well, hel-*lo*!' said one. The other turned and said to my sister: 'No trouble?' She shook her head. 'It's a wonder you couldn't be more careful,' she said angrily. 'They get out like that, how do *you* know what they're going to do?'

The man grunted and came over to me. 'Wanna come with us? I know somebody who's waiting to see you.'

I got up and walked slowly across the room, looking at the rug all the way, with one of the men on each side of me. When I got to the doorway beside my sister I pulled my hand out of the pocket of my coat and looked at it. I had one of my stones in my hand. It was very easy. Before either of them could stop me I reached out and stuffed the stone into her mouth. She screamed just before I touched her, and just afterward her lips were bleeding. But the whole thing took a very long time. Everybody was standing perfectly still. Next, the two men had hold of my arms very tight and I was looking around the room at the walls. I felt that my front teeth were broken. I could taste blood on my lips. I thought I was going to faint. I wanted to put my hand to my mouth, but they held my arms. This is the turning point, I thought.

I shut my eyes very hard. When I opened them everything was different and I knew I had won. For a moment I could not see very clearly, but even during that moment I saw myself sitting on the divan with my hands in front of my mouth. As my vision cleared, I saw that the men were holding my sister's arms, and that she was putting up a terrific struggle. I buried my face in my hands and did not look up again. While they were getting her out the front door, they managed to knock over the umbrella stand and smash it. It hurt her ankle and she kicked pieces of porcelain back into the hall. I was delighted. They dragged her along the walk to the car, and one man sat on each side of her in the back. She was yelling and showing her teeth, but as they left the city limits she stopped, and began to cry. All the same, she was really counting the service stations along the road on the way back to the Home, and she found there was one more of them than she had thought. When they came to the grade crossing near the spot where the train accident had happened, she looked out, but the car was over the track before she realized she was looking out the wrong side.

Driving in through the gate, she really broke down. They kept promising her ice-cream for dinner, but she knew better than to believe them. As she walked through the main door between the two men she stopped on the threshold, took out one of the stones from her coat pocket and put it into her mouth. She tried to swallow it, but it choked her, and they rushed her down the hall into a little waiting-room and made her give it up. The strange thing, now that I think about it, was that no one realized she was not I.

They put her to bed, and by morning she no longer felt like crying: she was too tired.

It's the middle of the afternoon and raining torrents. She is sitting on her bed (the very one I used to have) in the Home, writing all this down on paper. She never would have thought of doing that up until yesterday, but now she thinks she has become me, and so she does everything I used to do.

The house is very quiet. I am still in the living-room, sitting on the divan. I could walk upstairs and look into her bedroom if I wanted to. But it is such a long time since I have been up there, and I no longer know how the rooms are arranged. So I prefer to stay down here. If I look up I can see the square window of coloured glass over the stairs. Purple and orange, an hour-glass design, only the light never comes in very much because the house next door is so close. Besides, the rain is coming down hard here, too.

Julian Vreden

Roughly four decades ago New York newspapers carried the report of a domestic tragedy, poignant but unexceptional. A middle-aged husband and wife celebrated New Year's Eve by remaining quietly at home and joining in a suicide pact. They were found lying side by side on the floor of their living-room, each with an empty champagne glass near by. A partially empty bottle of champagne stood on the sink in the kitchen, along with a small amount of the cyanide which they had dissolved in the wine for their holiday libations. There were no explanatory notes.

The Vredens were both employees of the New York Board of Education. They had one son, Julian, not yet twenty, who had left Columbia and was now attending a college in Florida. The police must have entertained suspicions from the outset, but they played a slow game. Young Vreden collected the insurance from his father's policy, at which point he was unwise enough to appear with his friend Mark from Miami in the Park Avenue salesroom of a firm dealing in imported cars. He made a down payment on a particularly flamboyant Aston-Martin. The two young men were by then living in the apartment formerly occupied by the elder Vredens, both of them having dropped out of college, with no apparent intention of continuing their education. The police paid them a visit, and had no difficulty in getting Julian to admit that it was he who had administered the lethal champagne cocktails. Indeed, he made it clear that he considered himself amply justified in his behaviour.

His story, verified by relatives and neighbours (all of whom maintained a wholly unsympathetic attitude toward

him), was one of uninterrupted long-term parental persecu-
tion. Rather than being pleased that their son should have
spent his spare time reading, they were loudly contemptuous
of his literary interests. The reason: Julian read *poetry*. This
was unforgivable. The mother had a habit of looking into his
room and shouting: 'Look at the big sissy with his poetry!'
And his father, eyeing him with disgust, would groan: 'What
a fairy we've got for a son!' These constant attacks, year in
and year out, had no effect on the boy save to make him
increase defiantly the number of volumes of poetry with
which he filled his room.

The shift from Columbia to the Florida college clearly was
a desirable one from all points of view. The physical distance
between them must have served to mitigate somewhat the
permanent state of ill will between parents and son,
otherwise the surprise New Year's Eve telephone call and
subsequent visit would have been unthinkable. Perhaps they
thought he had changed, and were heartened by the prospect
of a possible armistice.

Julian arrived at the apartment alone, friend Mark having
agreed to wait outside in the corridor until Julian opened the
door for him. He had a bottle of Piper Heidsieck with him
which he uncorked in the kitchen and shared with them,
along with the conventional toasts to their good health
during the coming year. Then he took their empty glasses
back into the kitchen and refilled them, this time adding the
cyanide. When they staggered and dropped to the floor, he
opened the service door and let Mark into the kitchen. It was
when the elder Vreden looked up and saw the unfamiliar
grinning face behind his son that he uttered the only words
Julian remembered his father saying during the ordeal: 'Oh
God, who's that?'

When both victims were dead, Julian and Mark pushed the
bodies closer to one another, wiped the glasses clean, leaving
them on the rug near by, washed and put away the third
glass, and left the apartment to its New Year's Eve silence.
They flew back to Miami immediately.

The case was not one to attract a great deal of publicity: too
much time had elapsed between the murders and the
indictment. Julian and Mark were condemned to life impris-

onment in a New Jersey hospital for the criminally insane. Criminal? Yes. Insane? Not likely. The desire to avenge acts of injustice committed against one's person can scarcely be considered a sign of dementia. Julian Vreden's story is a classical and uniquely American tale of revenge.

If I Should Open My Mouth

Monday 26th ———

At last succeeded in finding the correct mixture of gum-arabic, sugar and essence of peppermint. Had the most complicated time getting Mrs Crawford out of the house and keeping her out for a sufficiently long time so that I could clean up the kitchen properly before she returned. I find this plan most exhilarating, however, and I intend to carry it through to its conclusion in the face of all obstacles. The subway station details are clear in my mind, and I have worked out the entire plan of action. In fact, the project is so extremely simple that it seems at times almost suspect. It is as if I were constantly being reassured by an invisible person whose face, if only I could see it, might easily prove to be wearing a falsely benign expression. However, it is only in the evenings that I begin to think of such things. A Seconal or two ought to arrange matters, at least for tonight, so that I can knit up some of that ravelled sleeve of care. Curious how disturbing the sound of a motorcycle can be out here in the still night air. There has been one idling somewhere up the road for the past ten minutes, popping and sputtering in a way calculated to drive a listener crazy. When it finally purred off into the distance it was like a relief from a constant pain. Why were machines ever invented? And what is this strange calm confidence that mankind has placed in these senseless toys it has managed to put together? That question I don't expect ever to be able to answer. I can only say that I know it is wrong.

Wednesday 28th ———

More complications, getting rid of Mrs C. while I dipped the tablets. The rest, gluing the ends of the boxes and so on, can be done up here in my room. A ridiculous facet of my feeling about all this is that while I am quite aware of the reprehensible aspects of my silly little project, for some unfathomable reason I feel hugely righteous about it all – more satisfyingly virtuous than I have in years. A quirk of human nature, I suppose.

Saturday 1st ———

I don't know why it is that ideas never occur to me except when I lack the time to put them down or when it is literally impossible to do so, as for instance when I am seated in a dentist's chair or surrounded by talking people at a dinner party, or even sound asleep, when often the best things come to light and are recognized as such by a critical part of my mind which is there watching, quite capable of judging but utterly unable to command an awakening and a recording. Sick-bed and fever often bring up astonishing things, but again, to what avail? A less ingenuous man than I might ask just why it should be of any importance to me that what goes on inside my mind should be put down. I am not a literary person and I never expect to be one, nor have I any intention of showing my notebooks to my friends. But that is a point not even to be discussed; long ago I determined to extract from my mind whatever by-products it could furnish. I have done it, I am still doing it, and I expect to continue to do it. The only difficulty is that whatever I am able to catch hold of is captured only after engaging in the most elaborate intrigues with my mind, playing hide-and-seek with various parts of it, exhausting myself in inventing disguises with which to surprise it, and in general having a most unpleasant time. Such as this very moment, this very page. A typical example of an occasion when there is not a single idea in view on the vast inner horizon. I am using up pages of my notebook, minutes when I might be strolling on the beach smelling the sea, in scribbling these absurd excuses, inventing alibis for not living, trying to find one more reason why I should feel justified in keeping these nonsensical journals year after year. Year after year, and life does not last for ever, not even an unsatisfactory one like mine. Perhaps this is the very thing which is keeping my life so unsatisfactory. If I could argue myself into stopping it all, even into destroying the notebooks, would it be better? Yes. Each minute would be complete in itself, like a room with four walls in which one can stand, sit, move about. Each day would be like a complete city shining in the sun, with its streets, parks and crowds. And the years would be whole countries to roam in. That much is certain. But the whole? That is to say, the interstices in time, the tiny chinks in consciousness when the total is there, enveloping one, and one knows that life is not made of time any more than the world is made of space. They would still occur, and they would be illicit because there would have been no arrangements made for them. What a man can distil and excrete will necessarily have some value for him (if only for him, as in my case) because its essence is of the interstices in time. One more justification, as idiotic as all the others, of the need for living an unsatisfactory life.

It seems to me that if one could accept existence as it is, partake of it fully, the world could be magical. The cricket on my balcony at the moment, piercing the night repeatedly with its hurried needle of sound, would be welcome merely because it is there, rather than an annoyance because it distracts me from what I am trying to do. Here I am, a man of fifty-five, who enjoys a certain respect on the part of his friends, cursing a small black insect outside the window. But I dare say all this is merely procrastination. I am probably trying to put off writing down what is really on my mind. It must go down, of course, because everything must go down, and truthfully. (I thought the cricket had stopped just then, but it has started again, quite the same as before.) I delivered the first twenty boxes today.

Sunday 2nd ———
The cricket got to be too much for me last night. It seemed to keep increasing its tempo, although I don't know how it could have managed to chirp any faster than it had been doing at the beginning. In any case, when I put down the great fact, I waited a while trying to decide how to go about

describing the distribution. Nothing untoward happened, it is quite true, while I was making the deliveries, but still, it seemed to me last night in my overwrought condition that a special effort was required for me to be able to go into the details. And while I waited, the cricket went on and on and on, faster and faster, or so it seemed to me, until it would have been impossible to set down another word. This morning, however, I am in fine shape.

It was raining a little when I started out, a warm, fine summer drizzle. One of the things I have noticed about myself since Anna and I split up is the fact that I have a sneaking fondness for walking in the rain without rubbers or a hat. Doubtless this is a predilection I have always had without realizing it, since first it was Mother and then Anna who always seemed somehow to prevent me from indulging in it. Quite rightly, too; I should probably have caught pneumonia and died long before this if it had not been for them. But since Anna left me and I have been here in Manor Heights alone, I occasionally slip out bareheaded and without rubbers, if the rain is not too heavy. Mrs Crawford, like a good housekeeper, has sometimes caught me at it, and brought it to my attention, hurrying to supply the needed accessories and thus obliging me to wear them. Yesterday morning, however, I managed to get out of the front door while she was in the kitchen talking to the delivery man from Macy's. I knew he would be coming, and I had everything ready, the twenty little boxes in the left-hand pocket of my jacket, the pennies in the right-hand trouser-pocket. The only way to do anything is to have it so well rehearsed in one's imagination that when the moment comes one does it automatically, as though for the hundredth time. Then it is all natural, and there is little likelihood of a slip-up. And there was no slip-up anywhere along the way. It was a heavy day, but not too hot because of the rain, which fell quietly as I walked down the road to the station. On the train I was not in the slightest degree perturbed: I knew there was no chance of any trouble. I kept marvelling at the peculiar pleasure afforded by the knowledge that one has planned a thing so perfectly there can be no room for the possibility of failure, all the while being conscious that both the pleasure and the idea itself were completely childish, and that my conviction of success was, at the very least, ill-founded. But certain situations call forth certain emotions, and the mind is a thing entirely apart. I have cakes of soap that I bought twenty-five years ago, still in their wrappers, and I am saving them in the perfect confidence that the right day will come to unwrap each one and use it. And there are probably a hundred books downstairs in the library that I am eager to read, have been eager to read for years, yet refuse to read until the day comes, the day that says to me: This is the morning to start Villiers de l'Ile Adam, or George Borrow, or Psichari, or someone else. Now, in my logical mind, I know quite well that these promised days are not likely ever to arrive: I shall never use those old cakes of soap that are stored in the linen closet, and I am reasonably sure of never reading *Romany Rye*, because it doesn't interest *me*. But there is that other person, the ideal one that I ought to be, and whom it does interest, and it comforts me to think that those things are there waiting for him. Certainly, the mind is a thing absolutely apart.

From the Grand Central I took the shuttle across to Times Square, then walked underground to the Eighth Avenue Subway. I chose the Independent as my territory, because of the great length of the stations. The air in that tube was almost steamy, and smelled of wet cement, hot metal and sewage. I took an express all the way up to Fort Tryon, worked slowly down through Harlem and then all the way to Canal Street. There was no hitch, no real difficulty, anywhere. The only place where there was even a meeting of any sort was at Twenty-third Street, where a coloured woman who was standing near the machine came up behind me as I was reaching in to take out the real package, which of course made it impossible for me to put in the one I held in my left hand. I did not hesitate for a fraction of a second. It was my determination that everything be carried off perfectly. I turned aside, put my left hand back into my coat-pocket, and proceeded to open the little box, shake out its two white candy-coated pellets into my hand and pop them into my mouth. If I were to suggest to anyone that this was an excellent piece of strategy, it would sound laughable, and yet it required quick thinking and a certain courage. In the first place, I have never chewed gum, and the idea of it disgusts me. (It occurs to me now that this distaste may easily have had some bearing on my choice of method for carrying out my project.) But much more than that secondary consideration was the fact that my co-ordination is not always of the best. On occasion it takes terrific concentration for me to distinguish right from left. And a second before, I had held in my left hand the *other* box, one of *my* boxes. What if, I said to myself, through some dark perversity of the subconscious, I should somehow have opened the wrong box? And as I crunched through the enamel walls of mint-sugar I found myself wondering if what I was tasting were the normal flavour, or whether it might be my flavour, my special mixture. I did not wait to get at that machine again, but continued downtown, skipping the West Fourth Street station because of the central platforms and the undesirable placing of the machines.

At Canal Street I had the pleasure of actually seeing the bait snapped up. I had no sooner put the penny in, retrieved the untouched box, and placed one of mine at the back of the shelf, when a young girl (Italian, I think) pushed past me and worked the machine. There was an expression of amusement on her face as she rejoined her friends at the edge of the platform. 'Gee, I'm gettin' good,' she said. 'I got two.'

I delivered the three final boxes in Brooklyn, returned to Manhattan, had a light meal at a Longchamps on Madison Avenue, and came home, feeling that the day had certainly not been wasted. I venture to say that I am embarked on the biggest comedy to be played in the subways of New York until the day Russia's superbombs lay them all bare to the sun. This is an infantile pastime I have devised, but at the same time it carries its own weight, and thus must have a meaning. However, I paid for my jaunt with a feeling of considerable fatigue, mostly of nervous origin, I suppose. Naturally, it was something of a strain. On an ordinary evening a cricket would not have been able to disturb me. Mrs. Crawford was indignant about the rubbers and the hat and the fact that my clothes were quite damp, of course. She is a good old soul. Today I have done nothing but sit in the garden reading the *Sunday Times*. The sun was out and in, all day, but it was not too hot.

This morning the Stewarts very kindly invited me on a picnic to Rye Beach. I could not entertain the thought of going, certainly. It's bad enough to have them living next door, to have to hear their abominable radio at all hours of the day and night, and put up with the depredations wrought in the garden by that untrained brat of theirs, without going out of my way to accompany them on an outing. It was a kind thought, however, and I have decided to go downtown the first thing tomorrow morning and buy a toy of some sort for little Dorothy. Maybe a tricycle, or something that will keep her on the sidewalk. Anywhere, anywhere, out of my garden!

Monday 3rd ———
I scarcely dared open the paper this morning, for fear of what I should find. Still, reading of the consequences is most assuredly a part of the procedure, and so I went ahead. But for some reason the police are keeping it quiet. There was nothing, anywhere. This silence managed to make me feel uncomfortable; in a way I feel as though I were being watched.

The Stewarts were most pleased with the velocipede, or whatever the chromium-plated contraption is called. Little Dorothy seemed quite overwhelmed by its splendour. As yet I have not seen her use it. I dare say she is too small to pull it by herself, up and down the two flights of steps between the front door and the sidewalk. I imagine for a while her parents will have to take it up and down for her.

Thursday 6th ———
The newspapers continue to maintain a stubborn silence, being filled instead with asinine stories about the electoral campaign. As if it could possibly change the course of history which of the two scarecrows gets into the seat of power. It was already too late to do that a hundred and seventy-five years ago. Too late to avert the sheer, obscene horror that has been on its way ever since, and is nearly here now. Voltaire, Marx, Roosevelt, Stalin, what were they but buds along the branch, like sores that have a way of bursting through the skin where it is thinnest? Who planted the tree of poison, who infected the blood? I am not qualified to say; the

complexities of the question are endless. But I believe that one of the culprits was our friend Rousseau. That unpardonable mechanism, the intellect, has several detestable aspects. Perhaps the worst is the interpenetration of minds; the influence, unconscious, even, that one mind can have over millions, is unforeseeable, immeasurable. You never know what form it will take, when it will make itself manifest.

Saturday 8th ——
The police assuredly are playing some sort of game. There must have been at least fifteen deaths, and not a word about one of them has appeared. That of course is their business, but I am amused and a little mystified to see how they are conducting it. Mrs C. has a heavy summer cold. I tried hard to make her stay in bed, but she is the soul of conscientiousness, and insists on continuing with her regular work.

Sunday 9th ——
It is an odd thing, that part of the mind which invents dreams and retains them, sometimes making of a certain dream a coloured lens, as it were, which comes between one's consciousness and one's vision of what passes for reality. That is, the feeling of the dream can remain when every detail has been lost. For several days now a particular atmosphere, taste, sensation, or whatever it may be called, has been haunting me. It can only be a dream-vestige, yet in spite of the fact that I have forgotten the dream it is very strong. And since it is gone it is unlocatable in time. It may have been this week or many years ago that the dream itself took place. The feeling, if it can be put into words at all, is one connected with languor, forgetfulness, lostness, emptiness, endlessness – one thing which would be all those things. Living my life and thinking my thoughts through that lens makes for a certain melancholy. I have tried desperately to find a door into the dream; perhaps if I could recall it, get back there, I could destroy its power. It is often a way. But it is almost as if it were an entity in itself, aware of my efforts to find it, and determined to remain hidden. As I feel I am approaching it I seem to sense a springing away, a definite recoil into some airless, unreachable region within. I don't like it: it worries me.

Monday 10th ———

When things become wholly unbelievable, all one can do is laugh. There is nothing to fall back upon but the bare fact of one's existence; one must forsake logic for magic. Because it was raining this morning (a morning rather like the day of my excursion to the city) and I wanted to take a short stroll, I went to the clothes closet and took out my grey flannel suit. I was entirely dressed when I suddenly recalled that there was a large hole in the right trouser-pocket. A strange feeling of confusion came over me, even before I started to think. But then the mental process commenced. How had the pennies stayed in my pocket that day? It was quite simple. I had changed my suit; now I remembered clearly taking off the grey flannel and putting on the herring-bone tweed. Perhaps if I had been able to live completely in the mind at that moment, I should have given it no further thought, and the unacceptable discovery would not have been made – at least, not then. But evidently I could not be satisfied with anything so simple. Another reflex sent my left hand to the pocket of the jacket, and that was the instant of my undoing. Later I took them all out and counted them sitting on the bed, but then I merely stood still, my hand inside the pocket feeling the jumble of small cardboard boxes, my mouth hanging open like an idiot's. It was inescapable – they were there. A second later I said aloud: 'Oh.' And I rushed over to the bureau drawer and opened it, because I wanted to be sure that these were not the untouched boxes I had collected. But they too were there, scattered among the piles of clean handkerchiefs. Then the others . . .? There is nothing to think. I *know* I delivered them.

At least, I believe I know. If I am to doubt my own eyes and ears, then it is time I gave up entirely. But in connection with that idea a ghastly little thought occurs to me: am I doubting my eyes and ears? Obviously not; only my memory. Memory is a cleverer trickster by far. In that case, however, I am stark, raving mad, because I remember every detail of those hours spent in the subway. But here are the boxes piled in front of me on the desk, all twenty. I know them intimately. I glued down each little flap with the maximum of care. There is no mistaking them. It is a shattering experience, and I feel ill, ill in every part of my being. A voice in me says: 'Accept the impossible. Leave off trying to make this fit in with your preconceived ideas of logic and probability. Life would be a sad affair if it reserved no surprises at all.' 'But not this sort!' I reply. 'Nothing quite so basically destructive of my understanding of the world!' I am going to bed. Everything is all wrong.

3.15 a.m. ———

The dream has emerged from its wrappings of fog. Not all of it, but that does not matter. I recognized it immediately when only a piece of it appeared, as I was lying here in the dark, half asleep. I relaxed and let more of it come. A senseless dream, it would seem, and yet powerful enough to have coloured all these past few days with its sadness. It is almost impossible to put down, since nothing *happens* in it: I am left only with vague impressions of being solitary in the park of some vast city. Solitary in the sense that although life is going on all around me, the cords that could connect me in any way with that life have been severed, so that I am as alone as if I were a spirit returned from the dead. Traffic moves past at some distance from where I am reclining on the ground under the trees. The time – timeless. I know there are streets full of people behind the trees, but I will never be able to touch them. If I should open my mouth to cry out, no sound would come forth. Or if I should stretch my arms towards one of the figures that occasionally wanders along the path near by, that would have no effect, because I am invisible. It is the terrible contradiction that is. unbearable: being there and yet knowing that I am not there, for in order to *be*, one must not only be to one's self: it is absolutely imperative that one be for others. One must have a way of basing one's being on the certainty that others know one is there. I am telling myself that somewhere in this city Mrs Crawford is thinking of me. If I could find her, she would be able to see me, and could give me a sign that would mean everything was all right. But she will never come by this place. I am hidden. I cannot move, I was born here, have always been here under these trees on this wet grass. And if I was born, perhaps I can die, and the city making its roar out beyond this park will stop being. That is my only hope. But it will take almost for ever. That is about all there is to the dream. Just that static picture of sadness and lostness.

The boxes are still there on my desk. They at least are no dream!

That little Dorothy is a horror. This evening at dusk I was returning from a short walk. It was nearly dark, and for some reason the street-lights had not yet been put on. I turned into the front walk, climbed up the steps, and had almost reached the house, when I banged full force into her damned tricycle. I am afraid my anger ran away with me, for I deliberately gave it such a push that it bumped all the way down both flights of steps and ran out into the middle of the street. A truck coming down the hill finished it off in a somewhat spectacular fashion. When I got inside I found the child in the kitchen talking with Mrs C. I did not mention the incident, but came directly upstairs.

It is a lovely evening. After dinner I am going to take all forty boxes to the woods behind the school and throw them on to the rubbish heap there. It's too childish a game to go on playing at my age.

Unwelcome Words

I

I'm glad you replied to my letter from the blue, although sorry to see that you imagine I think of you as a captive audience merely because you're confined to your room. Or was that said simply to make me feel guilty for having remained mobile?

Of course prices began to rise here long before the international oil blackmail of the seventies. We watched them go up, always thinking: They can't go any higher. Everything's five times as expensive as it was ten years ago. Since 1965 importation has been forbidden. So instead of imported goods we had smuggled goods, which fetched whatever people were willing to pay for them. (I suppose one should remember that prices here were incredibly low in the thirties and forties, so that they could keep on rising more or less indefinitely before they were equal to those of Europe or America. Then came the oil inflation, so that they're still going up, and still lower than other countries.)

Five years or so after independence, Christopher was talking with an old Berber somewhere in the south. In the midst of a general conversation the old man leaned toward him and said confidentially: 'Tell me. How long is this Independence going to go on?'

I remember in 1947 I sent to New York for a thousand dollars. (If you care to remember, that was enough to live on for three or four months in those days, at least here.) The bank where it was supposed to have been sent didn't have it, but they advised me to try all the other banks in town. There

46

were more than forty of them here then. I'd try two or three a day; nobody knew anything. A month later I still didn't have my money. The American Legation suggested I go to the first bank and demand it, at the same time hinting that the American Minister would take steps if they failed to produce it. Magic result: the clerk went straight to a filing cabinet and pulled out the cheque. But I've always wondered what they hoped to gain by holding it up for such a long time. (It seemed very long to me then, and I was indignant about it.) Now things are much worse. All foreign money coming into the country is thrown into a pool in Casablanca and kept there while interest is collected from those who borrow it, generally over a period of three months. Eventually the sum shows up on your bank statement, changed at whatever was the lowest rate during that period. It's perfectly understandable considering that the war goes on and is expensive, but that doesn't lessen the inconvenience. We're probably lucky not to have to pay a special war tax, and God knows, that may yet come. Sufficient unto the day.

You ask for news about me: my daily life, what I think about, my opinions on exterior events. All in good time, if I can do it. But what happens here in the city carries much more weight than what we hear from outside. There are plenty of crimes, but each year we seem to have one murder which interests everyone. The special interest lies in the victims having been non-Muslims. This fascinates Muslims as well as infidels, although doubtless for different reasons.

For instance, two years ago, while the workmen were still building the new mosque between here and the Place de France, an elderly woman used to appear from a building across the street, carrying pots of tea and coffee to the men. She'd come early in the morning, before sunrise, when the air was still cold, and the workmen looked forward to her arrival. One day she failed to appear, and later the same day they heard she'd been murdered in her bed. Someone had managed to climb up to her window and get into her apartment, and before leaving he had prudently cut her throat. He'd expected to find hidden money (which, the woman being Jewish, he naturally assumed he'd unearth somewhere). But she lived in poverty; he found nothing but a blue plastic transistor radio, and he took it. After that, although the workmen got no more tea or coffee, they had music from the blue transistor, but only for a few days. A neighbour of the murdered woman noticed the radio there among the mounds of tiles, and was so certain she had recognized it that she mentioned it to a policeman in the street. So of course they caught the workman, who said he wouldn't have cut the old Jewess's throat if he'd known how poor she was!

Then there was the case, last year, of the two old Americans (I don't think you ever knew them) who lived in a small house high up on the Old Mountain, at the very end of the navigable road, where it turns into what's left of the Roman road. They were truly isolated there, without a telephone or another house in sight. So after several decades of living up there in peace, they were suddenly attacked. The husband was in the garden at the edge of the woods, filling a ditch with water. The attackers felled him and pushed his head into the ditch. The wife saw everything through the window before they went into the house and beat her up, trying to make her tell where 'the money' was hidden. (These people were penniless, living on their Social Security cheques.) There was no money, so after landing a few more kicks in the woman's face, the marauders went on their way. The husband died; the wife survived. The incident alarmed the Europeans living on the Old Mountain Road, all of whom have large properties and are already guarded by night watchmen; the muggers chose the old couple precisely because they were unprotected, and of course got nothing at all out of it. The grapevine claims that the criminals were caught about two months later. They were part of a gang that lived in a cave on the coast to the west. But who knows? These things are taken more seriously by the European residents than food riots and battles with the so-called Polisario in the Sahara. The bridge-table mentality, if you'll pardon the slur.

So anyway, that's that for now.

II

Good that we're back in touch.

You're wrong; I do remember the last time we saw each other. You were living in that crazy apartment on the roof of the castle, and there was a terrible wind coming from the harbour. You had a few people there for dinner, and I remember the door on to the roof being opened and the wind blowing through the entire flat, so that everyone was calling out: 'Shut the door!' What the precise year was, I don't know, because the episode seems to have no context. The only other detail I recall is your remark that you couldn't read anything written after the eighteenth century. I accepted it as a personal idiosyncrasy; since then I've thought about it, wondering how healthy such a self-imposed stricture is for a twentieth-century author. Is it that you don't read contemporary writing any longer in order to escape from its possibly pernicious influence, or that any contact with present-day fiction is repugnant to you because it suggests the idea of competition? Of course your reasons for excluding the nineteenth century remain unexplained in any case. Although in music I could easily make a similar sweeping statement, relegating to oblivion all the music of the nineteenth century. But that kind of generalization is never fruitful, it seems to me, and I wonder how closely you adhere to your dictum.

Half the time I haven't even been sure where you were during these past fifteen years or so. Through others I heard you'd been living in Hong Kong, Tokyo and even Malaysia. (There was a town there which you were said to be fond of, but I can't remember its name. On the east coast, and fairly far north.) Once you'd got out of the habit of writing to me, you no longer knew where to write, which is understandable. The excuse applies even more strongly to me, since you had no fixed residence, whereas I always had a home base.

I needn't ask you if you remember Betty and Alec Howe, since they were your bridge and canasta partners, along with all the other residents I avoided knowing for years. Both of them died ten days or so ago; who knows of what? He first, and she a few days later. Smina is convinced that Betty did herself in so as not to have to go through Alec's funeral.

She could be right; I never knew the Howes except at parties and in the market. I suspect you won't bemoan their passing.

And of course there's the incredible Valeska. She's been back here several times since you have, although not in the past five years or so. Abdelouahaïd conceived a strong dislike for her, mainly because she steadfastly refused to sit in the front seat of the Mustang, even though it was the only comfortable passenger's seat in the car. Her insistence upon riding in back rubbed him the wrong way, since he assumed, and probably quite correctly, that she wanted to make it clear to the public that he was the chauffeur. This basic antipathy made it easy for him to criticize other facets of her behaviour. This he constantly did to me, but of course not to her. Then one day he found his chance and sprang. The result was so insane that I couldn't upbraid him afterwards as I should have.

On the days when I went to fetch Valeska at the hotel she always sat by a table in the courtyard, reading, doing crossword puzzles or whatever, but very busy. Abdelouahaïd would drive right up to the head of the stairs so she couldn't help seeing us, and she always glanced up once, so that it was certain she'd noticed. For some reason I couldn't fathom, she never budged until I got out of the car and went down into the courtyard and crossed it and stood within a foot of her table. This was a sacred rite. One day I stayed at home and sent Abdelouahaïd for her. When she saw him going down into the courtyard she jumped up and followed him up to the car, he said, asking again and again: 'Where's Paul? Where's Paul?'

At this point Satan must have arrived and prompted Abdelouahaïd to look at the ground and say sadly: 'Paul's dead.' You'll be able to imagine the screeches and squawks that followed on this announcement. He helped her into the car and they set off for Itesa. As you know, he doesn't speak English, but he knew enough words to convey to her that I was lying on the floor, and that people were standing around looking at me.

He said that as they got to the Plaza del Kuweit, Valeska suddenly cried out: 'Oh Christ! My camera's at the hotel. Never mind. Go on.'

She was literally hysterical when she saw me, safe and sound, and I thought: This is too much, and saw myself taking her to Beni Makada to the psychiatrist. Then she wheeled and shrieked at Abdelouahaïd: 'You son of a bitch!'

I don't think she's ever forgiven him for his joke, but he's still delighted by the memory of it. As I say, I couldn't bring myself to criticize him, since in a way he did it for me, thinking that she might change her behaviour as a result. But naturally it changed nothing, she considering it merely an arbitrary action by a crazy Arab who was curious to see how she'd react.

They're building fancy villas all around me. They're well built but hideous, and look like old-fashioned jukeboxes, their façades plastered with wrought iron and tile work. Each one is required by law to have a chimney, but in no case is the chimney connected with anything inside the house, being purely decorative. The builders are waiting for buyers who don't arrive. Will they ever? The prices seem very high: between $125,000 and $200,000 and there's no heat, of course – no furnace, no fireplaces – and often no space outside for a garden. Yet it's that space which determines whether they're to be considered officially villas, or merely houses (which don't have to have chimneys).

I hope all's well with you, and that you'll reply.

III

I've made it an objective to write you regularly if not frequently, to keep you in touch with this section of the outside world; it may help to aerate your morale. Clearly the only way to give you an idea of my life is for me to write whatever comes into my head. In the conscious selection of material to include, there is the possibility of imposing a point of view, a *parti pris*. I think my procedure will give you a more accurate picture of my daily life – at least, that part of it which goes on inside my head, by far the most important part.

I've often imagined being in your unenviable situation in the event of a fire or an earthquake. Not to be able to get out of your bed and try to run to safety. Or if you're in your wheelchair, not to be able to go anywhere in it save up and down the corridors. I think that would be my main preoccupation but again, maybe it wouldn't, since one doesn't live in constant expectation of fires and earthquakes. But I can see myself lying awake at night imagining in detail what it would be like to be asphyxiated by smoke or suddenly flung to the floor with a girder on top of my legs and the dust of plaster choking me. I hope you don't do that, and I somehow doubt that you do. By now you must have become enough of a fatalist to be able to consider all objective phenomena as concomitants of your condition. If that's the case, it may be partially due to your having had to put up for eight years with an impossible wife – a kind of training for the ultimate attainment of a state of total acceptance. At the same time it has occurred to me that the constant presence of a woman like Pamela may easily have augmented the tension which led eventually to the stroke. You suffered unnecessarily for those eight years. Pamela was a racist. She felt she operated on a higher level than yours because she was aware that three hundred years ago her ancestors were living in Massachusetts, whereas yours were living in some benighted region of the Ukraine. 'We were here first, so of course it's ours, but we love to have you here, because it makes life more interesting.' Am I wrong, or was Pamela like that? Weren't you always aware of a profound contradiction between what she said and the way she acted? At this great remove, I don't remember her very well. That is to say, her face escapes me; I can't project an image of it. I do remember her voice, however. It was beautifully modulated and a pleasure to listen to, except when she was angry. This was to be expected: one purposely changes one's voice and delivery as a means of communicating one's emotion. Yet now I have to ask: was Pamela *ever* angry? When I replay the mental tape I have of the breakfast in Quito (in that crazy ice-cream parlour with the balcony where they served food) I hear those trenchant staccato phrases of hers not as expressions of annoyance but as orders being given to an inferior. They had the desired effect: you shrank into your shell and said no more. Everything was delightful as long as there was no resistance; then commands had to be issued.

The truth is that for two or three decades I haven't thought of her at all. I thought of her this morning only because I was trying, from what I knew of your life, to imagine possible causes of a cerebral lesion. I admit that after the fact it's of purely academic interest. The autopsy doesn't cure the patient.

After I woke up this morning I recalled a silly song I heard as a child, when it was sung to me by a woman named Ethel Robb. (I don't know who she was, but I seem to remember that she was a schoolteacher.) The words struck me as so strange that I learned them by heart.

> In der vintertime ven der valley's green
> And der vind blows along der vindowsill
> Den der vomen in der vaudeville
> Ride der velocipedes around der vestibule.

(The melody was a variant of 'Ach, du lieber Augustin'.) Surely you never heard the song. I wonder if anyone ever did, outside Miss Robb's circle of acquaintances.

The early twenties was the time for absurd lyrics: witness 'Oh by Jingo', 'The Ogo Pogo', 'Lena Was the Queen of Palestina', 'Yes, We Have No Bananas', 'Barney Google' and God knows what else. There was also a Fanny Brice song called 'Second-hand Rose', which got me into trouble with the mother of my hostess when I sang it at a party here in the sixties. She paid no attention to: 'Even the piano in the parlour Papa bought for ten cents on the dollar.' But when I got to 'Even Abie Cohen, that's the boy I adore, had the nerve to tell me he'd been married before', the lady jumped up and ran across to the divan where I was sitting. She seized my face between her thumb and fingers and squeezed, crying: 'Even you, Paul Bowles, even you?' It was all so sudden and dramatic that I felt I'd committed a major solecism. Fortunately there were other guests who knew the song, and they were able to convince her that I hadn't been extemporizing for the occasion, although she didn't seem completely mollified.

I think the most important characteristic you and I have in common (although you'd be within your rights in claiming that we have no points at all in common) is a conviction that the human world has entered into a terminal period of disintegration and destruction, and that this will end in a state of affairs so violent and chaotic as to make any attempts at maintaining government or order wholly ineffective. I've always found you excoriating the decay of civilization even more vehemently than I. This of course was when the worst we could imagine was destruction by nuclear warfare. But now we can imagine conditions under which sudden death by fire might be a welcome release from the inferno of life; we might long for a universal euthanasia. Can we *hope* for nuclear war – I mean ethically – or are we bound out of loyalty to wish for the continuation of the human species at no matter what costs in suffering? I used the word ethical because it seems to me that unethical desires are bound to engender false conclusions.

I suppose what is at the bottom of my mind in all this is that I'm curious to know whether being totally incapacitated has altered your point of view in any way. Has it left you angrier, more resigned, or entirely indifferent? (Although that you never were, under any circumstances, so that I doubt the likelihood of such a major alteration in personality.) I have a feeling that you may consider these things a purely private matter, and as a result may resent my prurient probing.

IV

I can see that you don't really remember the weekend you referred to earlier. There's nothing shameful about not having total recall: still, it seems doubly unfortunate that you should have been deprived of both external *and* internal mobility: I mean the freedom to wander in the past, to explore the closets of memory. I know, it was forty years ago and you say you don't remember, that all three of us were so drunk none of us could possibly recall the details of that absurd excursion. But neither you nor I was drunk when we

arrived in the village (and had to get off the train because that
was as far as they'd built the railroad). It was still daylight,
and we crossed the river on that unfinished bridge to get to
the so-called hotel. Surely you remember that there was
nothing to drink but mescal; you kept saying that it smelled
like furniture polish, which as I recall it did. Have you ever
drunk any since? And what a night, with Bartolomé sitting
there getting drunker and drunker and giggling his head off.
And at one point (search well – you must remember this) the
mosquito net over my bed collapsed on to my head so that I
was swathed in folds of netting, and the dust made me
sneeze, and Bartolomé in his chair pointed at me while I
struggled, and cried: *Pareces al Niño Dios!* And you and he
laughed interminably while I sneezed and flailed my arms,
trying to find an opening in the net. By then there was
nothing to do but send Bartolomé down for another bottle of
Tehuacan and go on drinking our mescal. I think it was he
who finally extricated me from the netting. I admit that you
were more or less intoxicated, but certainly not enough so to
have drawn a blank. All that was fun, and belongs on the
credit side of the ledger. As usual, however, I was more
conscious of the unpleasant details than of all the amusement.
The next day was eternal. It was agony to be on that
plunging rattletrap little train, and I looked with loathing at
the miles of cactus on the parched hillsides. Each jolt of the
train increased the pounding in my head. Bartolomé slept.
You seemed to have no hangover, for which I felt some
bitterness; but then, you were used to alcohol and I was not.
But since you say you don't remember, I'm left alone with
the memory; I might as well have dreamed it all.

Sometimes I suspect you of exaggerating your present
deficiencies, not, certainly, to evoke pity, since that would be
unlike you, and besides, the desire to exaggerate is probably
unconscious in its origin. Nevertheless, you do emphasize
your unfortunate situation, so that one can't help feeling
sorry for you. The question is: Why do you italicize your
misfortune? My feeling is that it's simply out of bitterness. I
feel you thinking: Now I'm in a wheelchair. That's that, and
that's what the world wanted. In other words *they* have done
it to you. If only you were religious, you could blame it on

God, or wouldn't that be any more satisfactory? As I remember, you're not particularly fond of animals. I've always been an ailurophile myself as opposed to a dog-lover. It seemed to me there'd be time enough later to make friends with the canines. Here there's not much likelihood of that. At night they're out in packs, and sometimes attack passers-by in the street. A sextet of them chased an American friend for a quarter of a mile one evening along the new road that goes from the foot of the Old Mountain to the new section of Dradeb. When one particular dog gets to be a continuous sleep-disturber I've twice resorted to drastic measures. It would be better to describe the drastic measures, I realize, than let you think that I poisoned the beasts. Naturally that was the first thing that occurred to me, but I decided against it because of the suffering it causes. Also, the symptoms of death from rat poison (the only lethal product I'd have been able to find here) are so classical that the owner of the animal would immediately suspect that his watchdog had been poisoned. My system with the first brute, which used to bark all night from the garden next door, was time-consuming but effective. It involved my staying up half the night for a week in my wait for a completely deserted street. About half-past one I would go to the kitchen and prepare the half pound of raw hamburger. One night I would mix Melleril and Largactyl with the meat, the following night I would grind up several tablets of Anafranil. I continued the alternation until the dog's owner decided it was rabid, and had it shot. There was no more barking after the first night of treatment. This seemed the most humane way of getting rid of the animal.

Another year a bitch whelped in the garage, which is always open. The night watchman gave her a carton to lie in with her pups. When these had been given away, she remained in the garage, encouraged by an eccentric Ethiopian woman who sent her maid at all hours with food for her. As soon as she felt thoroughly at home in the garage, she began to engage in long-distance conversations with friends in Ain Hayani and Dradeb. I complained about this to Abdelouahaïd; I thought he might have a solution. He had a very simple one. He picked up the bitch and put her into the boot of the car. We drove to the Forêt Diplomatique, to the edge of the beach, where there's a restaurant run by a Moroccan with a crew of dogs. Before letting her out of the boot, Abdelouahaïd turned the Mustang around, to be able to start up quickly. She stood on the beach for a second, bewildered; the other dogs saw her and came to investigate. While they surrounded her Abdelouahaïd started up, and we escaped, even though I saw her running behind the car for a good distance as we drove through the woods. She wasn't stupid: as soon as she heard the motor she pushed the other dogs aside and rushed toward the car.

Something has happened to the Moroccans. Fifty years ago dogs were execrated. Only people living in the country owned them. Too dirty to live in the city. Somehow they noticed that practically all French women went into the street accompanied by dogs on leashes, and gradually began to imitate them. At first it was boys leading curs by ropes which they tied tightly around the animals' necks. French ladies passing by would be indignant. *Mais ce pauvre chien! Tu vas l'étrangler!* Now every Moroccan child in neighbourhoods such as mine has a canine pet. Most are German shepherds: fathers think they provide better protection.

The French are unpredictable. Last month a young photographer from Paris was here taking pictures for *Libération*. The only thing which moved him to exclamations of surprise was the size of a peanut-butter jar full of birdseed. Is that authentic? He wanted to know. Do they really sell such large jars of peanut-butter? When I said yes, I'm not sure he didn't suspect me of pulling his leg, as he went across the room and examined it carefully. Merry Christmas.

V

Someone sent me a box of American chocolate creams last week. On the cover are the words *Home Fashioned*. On another facet of the same cover is a list of ingredients included in the home-fashioning. Among these are: invert sugar, partially hydrogenated vegetable oils, sorbitol, lecithin, butylated hydroxytoluene, butylated hydroxyanisole, propyl gallate, potassium sorbate, sulphur dioxide and benzoate of soda. Even the most modern home isn't likely to have all these delicacies in its kitchen. Although I haven't been in an American kitchen in many years, I know that they're inclined to look more and more like laboratories. Perhaps by now they have chemical cabinets stocked with everything from triethylene glycol to metoclopramide.

The kitchens in farmhouses at the time of the First World War were not too pleasant to be in either, as I remember, in spite of all the propaganda romanticizing them. There were mingled odours of sour milk, dill and iron from the well water. Spirals of flypaper hung from every convenient hook, and the flies still buzzed on all sides. If there were dogs, they smelled. If there were children, they smelled. It was unbelievable that serious people should want to live that way. What's the matter with them? Nothing. They just don't know any better, that's all. This answer never satisfied me. It implied a double standard that made it possible for my parents to overlook these people's shortcomings. But they never forgave *me* for not knowing something I ought to know, and the severity was applied precisely because I was not a farm boy. Seventy years ago there existed that class difference between those brought up in the city and those brought up on the farm. Now there seems to be very little distinction made. The concept of class has been carefully destroyed. Either you have money or you don't. The result of democracy, I suppose, when it's misunderstood to mean similarity rather than equality.

You couldn't have known the typical small, medium-priced hotel of Paris in the twenties. (By the time you got to Paris, after the Second World War, things had changed somewhat.) There were only three or four rooms per floor, the staircases and corridors were heavily carpeted and the windows were hidden by two sets of curtains. Normally there were two lights in the room, one hanging from the centre of the ceiling and the other above the bed's headboard. Both were affixed to a system of pulleys, so that they could be propelled upward or downward according to the needs of the moment. The wallpaper was always dark with wide stripes in colours which might at one time have been garish, although there was no way of knowing, since the patina of age had long since darkened them. It was easy to feel encased and protected in those rooms, and I often dream about them even now. Such dreams, however, aren't pleasant, since I seem always to be on the point of having to leave in order to let someone else move in. No dream without at least subliminal anxiety.

Incidentally, you have no reason to upbraid me for not giving my specific reactions to your most recent tale of woe. Such reactions can only be emotional in content, and there's never any point in expressing emotions in words, it seems to me. I assure you, nevertheless, that I experienced a feeling of profound chagrin when I read your letter and realized that you were undergoing futher torments, and I thought I'd conveyed that impression earlier.

You may remember (although probably not, since you never crack a book written in our century) a phrase used by the Castor in *La Nausée*: '*Je me survis*' (ineptly translated in the American edition as 'I outlive myself'. I understand the Castor's feeling of being her own survivor; it's not unlike my feeling, save that I'd express mine as: 'Ma vie est posthume.' Do you make sense of that?

I've often wished that someone would rewrite the end of *Huckleberry Finn*, delivering it from the farcical closing scenes which Twain, probably embarrassed by the lyrical sweep of the nearly completed book, decided were necessary if the work were to be appreciated by American readers. It's the great American novel, damaged beyond repair by its author's senseless sabotage. I'd be interested to have your opinion, or do you feel that the book isn't worth having an opinion about, since a botched masterpiece isn't a masterpiece at all? Yet to counterfeit the style successfully, so that the break would be seamless and the prose following it a convincing continuation of what came before – that seems an impossible task. So I shan't try it, myself.

I think a warning sign of creeping senility is the shortening of the attention span, which strikes me as a form of regression to childhood. We'll see.

VI

I haven't mentioned the mounting hostility I've noted in your letters because I've assumed that it was directed at the world in general, and not at me. Now I see how mistaken I was. First you tell me that my letters are self-indulgent. I let that pass: it was merely a criticism of my method. But I can't overlook the word 'gloating'. On seeing that, I realize that I'd have done better to limit my correspondence to one necessarily cruel *Get Well* card, and let it go at that.

It seems to me that for this final period of your life it might be profitable to stop encouraging your masochistic tendencies. I can see that you don't feel that way at all, and that on the contrary you intend to go on giving free rein to them. Too bad. There's obviously nothing I can do from here to help you, so I may as well let it rest. But as you sink into your self-imposed non-being, I hope you'll remember (you won't) that I made this small and futile attempt to help you remain human.

Hasta el otro mundo, as Rosa Lopez used to say.

The Fourth Day Out from Santa Cruz

Ramón signed on at Cádiz. The ship's first call was at Santa Cruz de Tenerife, a day and a half out. They put in at night, soon after dark, Floodlights around the harbour illumined the steep bare mountains and made them grass-green against the black sky. Ramón stood at the rail, watching. 'It must have been raining here,' he said to a member of the crew standing beside him. The man grunted, looking not at the green slopes unnaturally bright in the electric glare, but at the lights of the town ahead. 'Very green,' went on Ramón, a little less certainly; the man did not even grunt in reply.

As soon as the ship was anchored, scores of Hindu shopkeepers came aboard with laces and embroidered goods for the passengers who might not be going ashore. They stayed on the first-class deck, not bothering to go down below to third-class where Ramón was scullery boy in the passengers' *cocina*. The work so far did not upset him; he had held more exacting and tiring jobs in Cádiz. There was sufficient food, and although it was not very good, nevertheless it was better than what was taken out to the third-class passengers. It had never occurred to Ramón to want privacy in his living quarters, so that he was unmoved by the necessity of sharing a cabin with a dozen or so shipmates. Still, he had been acutely unhappy since leaving Cádiz. Except for the orders they gave him in the kitchen, the sailors behaved as if he did not exist. They covered his bunk with their dirty clothes, and lay on it, smoking, at night when he wanted to sleep. They failed to include him in any conversation, and so far no one had even made an allusion, however deprecatory, to his existence. For them it appeared that he simply was not present. To even the least egocentric man such a state of affairs can become intolerable. In his sixteen years Ramón had not been in a similar situation; he had been maltreated but not wholly disregarded.

Most of the crew stood at the prow smoking, pointing out bars to one another, as they scanned the waterfront. Partly out of perversity born of his grievance, and partly because he wanted to be by himself for a spell, Ramón walked to the stern and leaned heavily against the rail, looking down into the darkness below. He could hear an automobile horn being blown continuously as it drove along the waterfront. The hills behind backed up the sound, magnified it as they threw it across the water. To the other side was the dim roar of the sea's waves against the breakwater. He was a little homesick, and as he stood there he became angry as well. It was inadmissible that this state of affairs should continue. A day and a half was too long; he was determined to force a change immediately, and to his undisciplined young mind kept recurring the confused image of a fight – a large-scale struggle with the entire crew, in which he somehow finished as the sole victor.

It is pleasant to walk by the sea-wall of a foreign port at night, with the autumn wind gently pushing at your back. Ramón was in no hurry; he stopped before each café and listened to the guitars and shouting, without, however, allowing himself to be detained by the women who called to him from the darker doorways. Having had to clean up the galley after an extra meal had been served to sixty workmen who had just come aboard here at Santa Cruz, bound for South America, he had been the last to get off the ship, and so he was looking for his shipmates. At the Café del Teide he found several of them seated at a table sharing a bottle of rum. They saw him come in, but they gave no sign of recognition. There was no empty chair. He walked toward the table, slowed down a bit as he approached it, and then continued walking toward the back of the café. The man behind the bar called out to him: 'You were looking for something?' Ramón turned around and sat down suddenly at a small table. The waiter came and served him, but he scarcely noticed what he was drinking. He was watching the table with the six men from his ship. Like one fascinated, he let his eyes follow each gesture: the filling of the little glasses, the tossing down the liquor, the back of the hand wiping the mouth. And he listened to their words punctuated by loud laughter. Resentment began to swell in him; he felt that if he sat still any longer he would explode. Pushing back his chair, he jumped up and strode dramatically out into the street. No one noticed his exit.

He began to walk fast through the town, paying no attention to where he was going. His eyes fixed on an imaginary horizon, he went through the *plaza,* along the wide Paseo de Ronda, and into the tiny streets that lie behind the cathedral. The number of people in the streets increased as he walked away from the centre of town, until when he had come to what seemed an outlying district, where the shops were mere stalls, he was forced to saunter along with the crowd. As he slowed down his gait, he felt less nervous. Gradually he took notice of the merchandise for sale, and of the people around him. It suddenly occurred to him that he would like to buy a large handkerchief. Outside certain booths there were wires strung up; from these hung, clipped by their corners, a great many of the squares of cloth, their bright colours showing in the flare of the carbide lamps. As Ramón stopped to choose one at the nearest booth he became aware that in the next booth a girl with a laughing face was also buying a bandanna. He waited until she had picked out the one she wanted, and then he stepped quickly over to the shopkeeper and pointing down at the package he was making, said: 'Have you another handkerchief exactly like that?' The girl paid no attention to him and put her change into her purse. 'Yes', said the shopkeeper, reaching out over the counter to examine the bandannas. The girl picked up her little packet wrapped in newspaper, turned away, and walked along the street. 'No, you haven't!' cried Ramón, and he hurried after her so as not to lose sight of her in the crowd. For some distance he trailed her along the thoroughfare, until

she turned into a side street that led uphill. It smelled here of
drains and there was very little light. He quickened his pace
for fear she would go into one of the buildings before he had
had the opportunity to talk to her. Somewhere in the back of
his mind he hoped to persuade her to go with him to the Café
del Teide. As he overtook her, he spoke quietly without
turning his head: 'Señorita.' To his surprise she stopped
walking and stood still on the pavement. Although she was
very near to him, he could not see her face clearly.

'What do you want?'

'I wanted to talk to you.'

'Why?'

He could not answer.

'I thought . . .' he stammered.

'What?'

There was a silence, and then as she laughed Ramón
remembered her face: open and merry, but not a child's face.
In spite of the confidence its recalled image inspired in him,
he asked: 'Why do you laugh?'

'Because I think you're crazy.'

He touched her arm and said boldly: 'You'll see if I'm
crazy.'

'I'll see nothing. You're a sailor. I live here'; she pointed to
the opposite side of the street. 'If my father sees you, you'll
have to run all the way to your ship.' Again she laughed. To
Ramón her laugh was music, faintly disturbing.

'I don't want to bother you. I only wanted to talk to you,'
he said, timid again.

'Good. Now you've talked. *Adios.*' She began to walk on.
So did Ramón, close beside her. She did not speak. A
moment later, he remarked triumphantly: 'You said you
lived back there!'

'It was a lie,' she said in a flat voice. 'I always lie.'

'Ah. You always lie,' echoed Ramón with great seriousness.

They came to a street light at the foot of a high staircase.
The sidewalk became a series of stone steps leading steeply
upward between the houses. As they slowly ascended, the air
changed. It smelled of wine, food cooking, and burning
eucalyptus leaves. Up above the city here, life was more
casual. People leaned over the balconies, sat in dark

doorways chatting, stood in the streets like islands among the moving dogs and children.

The girl stopped and leaned against the side of a house. She was a little out of breath from the climb.

'Tired?' he asked.

Instead of replying she turned swiftly and darted inside the doorway beside her. For a few seconds Ramón was undecided whether or not to follow her. By the time he had tiptoed into the dimly lit passageway she had disappeared. He walked through into the courtyard. Some ragged boys who were running about stopped short and stared at him. A radio was playing guitar music above. He looked up. The building was four storeys high; there were lights in almost all the windows.

On his way back to the waterfront a woman appeared from the shadows of the little park by the cathedral and took his arm. He looked at her; she was being brazenly coy, with her head tilted at a crazy angle as she repeated: 'I like sailors.' He let her walk with him to the Café del Teide. Once inside, he was disappointed to see that his shipmates were gone. He bought the woman a *manzanilla* and walked out on her as she began to drink it. He had not said a word to her. Outside, the night seemed suddenly very warm. He came to the Blanco y Negro; a band was playing inside. Two or three of the men from the ship were on the dark dance floor, trying to instil a bit of life into the tired girls that hung to them. He did not even have a drink here, but hurried back to the ship. His bunk was piled with newspapers and bundles, but the cabin was empty, and he had several hours in the dark in which to brood and doze, before the others arrived. The boat sailed at dawn.

They skirted the island next day – not close enough to see the shore, but within sight of the great conical mountain, which was there all day beside them in the air, clear in distant outline. For two days the ship continued on a south-west course. The sea grew calm, a deep blue, and the sun blazed brighter in the sky. The crew had ceased gathering on the poop-deck, save in the early evening and at night, when they lay sprawled all over it, singing in raucous voices while the stars swayed back and forth over their heads.

For Ramón life continued the same. He could see no difference in the crew's attitude toward him. It still seemed to him that they lived without him. The magazines that had been bought at Santa Cruz were never passed around the cabin. Afternoons when the men sat around the table in the third-class *comedor,* the stories that were recounted could never be interpreted by any gesture in their telling as being directed at a group that included him. And he certainly knew better than to attempt to tell any himself. He still waited for a stroke of luck that might impose him forcibly upon their consciousness.

In the middle of the fourth morning out from Santa Cruz he poked his head from the galley and noticed several of the men from his cabin gathered along the railing at the stern. The sun was blinding and hot, and he knew something must be keeping them there. He saw one man pointing aft. Casually he wandered out across the deck to within a few feet of the group, searching the sea and the horizon for some object – something besides the masses of red seaweed that constantly floated by on top of the dark water.

'It's getting nearer!'
'*Qué fuerza!*'
'It's worn out!'
'*Claro!*'

Ramón looked over their heads, and between them when they changed position from time to time. He saw nothing. He was almost ready to be convinced that the men were baiting him, in the hope of being able to amuse themselves when his curiosity should be aroused to the point of making him ask: 'What is it?' And so he was determined to be quiet, to wait and see.

Suddenly he did see. It was a small yellow and brown bird flying crookedly after the boat, faltering as it repeatedly fell back toward the water between spurts of desperate energy.

'A thousand miles from land!'
'It's going to make it! Look! Here it comes!'
'No!'
'Next time.'

At each wild attempt to reach the deck, the bird came closer to the men, and then, perhaps from fear of them, it fluttered down toward the boiling sea, missing the wake's maelstrom by an ever closer margin. And when it seemed that this time it surely would be churned under into the white chaos of air and water, it would surge feebly upward, its head turned resolutely toward the bright mass of the ship that moved always in front of it.

Ramón was fascinated. His first thought was to tell the men to step back a little from the rail so that the bird might have the courage to land. As he opened his mouth to suggest this, he thought better of it, and was immediately thankful for having remained quiet. He could imagine the ridicule that would have been directed at him later: in the cabin, at mealtime, evenings on the deck.... Someone would have invented a shameful little ditty about Ramón and his bird. He stood watching, in a growing agony of suspense.

'Five pesetas it goes under!'

'Ten it makes it!'

Ramón wheeled about and ran lightly across to the galley. Almost immediately he came out again. In his arms he carried the ship's mascot, a heavy tomcat that blinked stupidly in the sudden glare of the sun. This time he walked directly back to the railing where the others stood. He set the animal down at their feet.

'What are you doing?' said one.

'Watch,' said Ramón.

They were all quiet a moment. Ramón held the cat's flanks and head steady, waiting for it to catch sight of the fluttering bird. It was difficult to do. No matter how he directed its head it showed no sign of interest. Still they waited. As the bird came up to the level of the deck at a few feet from the boat, the cat's head suddenly twitched, and Ramón knew the contact had been made. He took his hands away. The cat stood perfectly still, the end of its tail moving slightly. It took a step closer to the edge, watching each movement of the bird's frantic efforts.

'Look at that!'

'He sees it.'

'But the bird doesn't see him.'

'If it touches the boat, the ten pesetas still go.'

The bird rose in the air, flew faster for a moment until it

was straight over their heads. They looked upward into the flaming sun, trying to shade their eyes. It flew still further forward, until, if it had dropped, it would have landed a few feet ahead of them on the deck. The cat, staring up into the air, ran quickly across the deck so that it was directly below the bird, which slowly let itself drop until it seemed that they could reach out and take it. The cat made a futile spring into the air. They all cried out, but the bird was too high. Suddenly it rose much higher; then it stopped flying. Swiftly they passed beneath it as it remained poised an instant in the air. When they had turned their heads back it was a tiny yellow thing falling slowly downward, and almost as quickly they lost sight of it.

At the noonday meal they talked about it. After some argument the bets were paid. One of the oilers went to his cabin and brought out a bottle of cognac and a set of little glasses which he put in front of him and filled, one after the other.

'Have some?' he said to Ramón.

Ramón took a glass, and the oiler passed the rest around to the others.

Pastor Dowe at Tacaté

Pastor Dowe delivered his first sermon in Tacaté on a bright
Sunday morning shortly after the beginning of the rainy
season. Almost a hundred Indians attended, and some of
them had come all the way from Balaché in the valley. They
sat quietly on the ground while he spoke to them for an hour
or so in their own tongue. Not even the children became
restive; there was the most complete silence as long as he kept
speaking. But he could see that their attention was born of
respect rather than of interest. Being a conscientious man he
was troubled to discover this.

When he had finished the sermon, the notes for which
were headed 'Meaning of Jesus', they slowly got to their feet
and began wandering away, quite obviously thinking of
other things. Pastor Dowe was puzzled. He had been assured
by Dr Ramos of the university that his mastery of the dialect
was sufficient to enable his prospective parishioners to follow
his sermons, and he had had no difficulty conversing with the
Indians who had accompanied him up from San Gerónimo.
He stood sadly on the small thatch-covered platform in the
clearing before his house and watched the men and women
walking slowly away in different directions. He had the
sensation of having communicated absolutely nothing to
them.

All at once he felt he must keep the people here a little
longer, and he called out to them to stop. Politely they
turned their faces toward the pavilion where he stood, and
remained looking at him, without moving. Several of the
smaller children were already playing a game, and were
darting about silently in the background. The pastor glanced

at his wrist-watch and spoke to Nicolás, who had been pointed out to him as one of the most intelligent and influential men in the village, asking him to come up and stand beside him.

Once Nicolás was next to him, he decided to test him with a few questions. 'Nicolás,' he said in his dry, small voice, 'what did I tell you today?'

Nicolás coughed and looked over the heads of the assembly to where an enormous sow was rooting in the mud under a mango tree. Then he said: 'Don Jesucristo.'

'Yes,' agreed Pastor Dowe encouragingly. '*Bai*, and Don Jesucristo what?'

'A good man,' answered Nicolás with indifference.

'Yes, yes, but what more?' Pastor Dowe was impatient; his voice rose in pitch.

Nicolás was silent. Finally he said, 'Now I go', and stepped carefully down from the platform. The others again began to gather up their belongings and move off. For a moment Pastor Dowe was furious. Then he took his notebook and his Bible and went into the house.

At lunch Mateo, who waited on table, and whom he had brought with him from Ocosingo, stood leaning against the wall smiling.

'Señor,' he said, 'Nicolás says they will not come again to hear you without music.'

'Music!' cried Pastor Dowe, setting his fork on the table. 'Ridiculous! What music? We have no music.'

'He says the father at Yalactín used to sing.'

'Ridiculous!' said the pastor again. 'In the first place I can't sing, and in any case it's unheard of! *Inaudito!*'

'*Sí, verdad?*' agreed Mateo.

The pastor's tiny bedroom was breathlessly hot, even at night. However, it was the only room in the little house with a window on the outside; he could shut the door on to the noisy patio where by day the servants invariably gathered for their work and their conversations. He lay under the closed canopy of his mosquito net, listening to the barking of the dogs in the village below. He was thinking about Nicolás. Apparently Nicolás had chosen for himself the role of envoy from the village to the mission. The pastor's thin lips moved.

'A troublemaker,' he whispered to himself. 'I'll speak with him tomorrow.'

Early the next morning he stood outside Nicolás's hut. Each house in Tacaté had its own small temple: a few tree trunks holding up some thatch to shelter the offerings of fruit and cooked food. The pastor took care not to go near the one that stood near by; he already felt enough like a pariah, and Dr Ramos had warned him against meddling of that sort. He called out.

A little girl about seven years old appeared in the doorway of the house. She looked at him wildly a moment with huge round eyes before she squealed and disappeared back into the darkness. The pastor waited and called again. Presently a man came around the hut from the back and told him that Nicolás would return. The pastor sat down on a stump. Soon the little girl stood again in the doorway; this time she smiled coyly. The pastor looked at her severely. It seemed to him she was too old to run about naked. He turned his head away and examined the thick red petals of a banana blossom hanging near by. When he looked back she had come out and was standing near him, still smiling. He got up and walked toward the road, his head down, as if deep in thought. Nicolás entered through the gate at that moment, and the pastor, colliding with him, apologized.

'Good,' grunted Nicolás. 'What?'

His visitor was not sure how he ought to begin. He decided to be pleasant.

'I am a good man,' he smiled.

'Yes,' said Nicolás. 'Don Jesucristo is a good man.'

'No, no, no!' cried Pastor Dowe.

Nicolás looked politely confused, but said nothing.

Feeling that his command of the dialect was not equal to this sort of situation, the pastor wisely decided to begin again. 'Hachakyum made the world. Is that true?'

Nicolás nodded in agreement, and squatted down at the pastor's feet, looking up at him, his eyes narrowed against the sun.

'Hachakyum made the sky,' the pastor began to point, 'the mountains, the trees, those people there. Is that true?'

Again Nicolás assented.

'Hachakyum is good. Hachakyum made you. True?'
Pastor Dowe sat down again on the stump.

Nicolás spoke finally, 'All that you say is true.'

The pastor permitted himself a pleased smile and went on.
'Hachakyum made everything and everyone because he is
mighty and good.'

Nicolás frowned. 'No!' he cried. 'That is not true!
Hachakyum did not make everyone. He did not make you.
He did not make guns or Don Jesucristo. Many things he did
not make!'

The pastor shut his eyes a moment, seeking strength.
'Good,' he said at last in a patient voice. 'Who made the other
things? Who made me? Please tell me.'

Nicolás did not hesitate. 'Metzabok.'

'But who is Metzabok?' cried the pastor, letting an
outraged note show in his voice. The word for God he had
always known only as Hachakyum.

'Metzabok makes all the things that do not belong here,'
said Nicolás.

The pastor rose, took out his handkerchief and wiped his
forehead. 'You hate me,' he said, looking down at the Indian.
The word was too strong, but he did not know how to say it
any other way.

Nicolás stood up quickly and touched the pastor's arm
with his hand.

'No. That is not true. You are a good man. Everyone likes
you.'

Pastor Dowe backed away in spite of himself. The touch of
the brown hand was vaguely distasteful to him. He looked
beseechingly into the Indian's face and said, 'But Hachakyum
did not make me?'

'No.'

There was a long pause.

'Will you come next time to my house and hear me speak?'

Nicolás looked uncomfortable.

'Everyone has work to do,' he said.

'Mateo says you want music,' began the pastor.

Nicolás shrugged. 'To me it is not important. But the
others will come if you have music. Yes, that is true. They
like music.'

'But *what* music?' cried the pastor in desperation.

'They say you have a *bitrola*.'

The pastor looked away, thinking: There is no way to keep anything from these people. Along with all his other household goods and the things left behind by his wife when she died, he had brought a little portable phonograph. It was somewhere in the store-room piled with the empty valises and cold-weather garments.

'Tell them I will play the *bitrola*,' he said, going through the gate.

The little girl ran after him and stood watching him as he walked up the road.

On his way through the village the pastor was troubled by the reflection that he was wholly alone in this distant place, alone in his struggle to bring the truth to its people. He consoled himself by recalling that it is only in each man's own consciousness that the isolation exists; objectively man is always a part of something.

When he arrived home he sent Mateo to the store-room to look for the portable phonograph. After a time the boy brought it out, dusted it and stood by while the pastor opened the case. The crank was inside. He took it out and wound the spring. There were a few records in the compartment at the top. The first he examined were 'Let's Do It', 'Crazy Rhythm', and 'Strike up the Band', none of which Pastor Dowe considered proper accompaniments to his sermons. He looked further. There was a recording of Al Jolson singing 'Sonny Boy' and a cracked copy of 'She's Funny That Way'. As he looked at the labels he remembered how the music on each disc had sounded. Unfortunately Mrs Dowe had disliked hymn music; she had called it 'mournful'.

'So here we are,' he signed, 'without music.'

Mateo was astonished. 'It does not play?'

'I can't play them this music for dancing, Mateo.'

'*Cómo nó, señor!* They will like it very much!'

'No, Mateo!' said the pastor forcefully, and he put on 'Crazy Rhythm' to illustrate his point. As the thin metallic tones issued from the instrument, Mateo's expression changed to one of admiration bordering on beatitude. '*Qué bonito!*' he said reverently. Pastor Dowe lifted the tone arm and the hopping rhythmical pattern ceased.

'It cannot be done,' he said with finality, closing the lid.

Nevertheless on Saturday he remembered that he had promised Nicolás there would be music at the service, and he decided to tell Mateo to carry the phonograph out to the pavilion in order to have it there in case the demand for it should prove to be pressing. This was a wise precaution, because the next morning when the villagers arrived they were talking of nothing but the music they were to hear.

His topic was 'The Strength of Faith', and he had got about ten minutes into the sermon when Nicolás, who was squatting directly in front of him, quietly stood up and raised his hand. Pastor Dowe frowned and stopped talking.

Nicolás spoke: 'Now music, then talk. Then music, then talk. Then music.' He turned around and faced the others. 'That is a good way.' There were murmurs of assent, and everyone leaned a bit further forward on his haunches to catch whatever musical sounds might issue from the pavilion.

The pastor sighed and lifted the machine on to the table, knocking off the Bible that lay at the edge. 'Of course,' he said to himself with a faint bitterness. The first record he came to was 'Crazy Rhythm'. As it started to play, an infant near by, who had been singsonging a series of meaningless sounds, ceased making its parrot-like noises, remaining silent and transfixed as it stared at the platform. Everyone sat absolutely quiet until the piece was over. Then there was a hubbub of approbation. 'Now more talk,' said Nicolás, looking very pleased.

The pastor continued. He spoke a little haltingly now, because the music had broken his train of thought, and even by looking at his notes he could not be sure just how far he had got before the interruption. As he continued, he looked down at the people sitting nearest him. Beside Nicolás he noticed the little girl who had watched him from the doorway, and he was gratified to see that she was wearing a small garment which managed to cover her. She was staring at him with an expression he interpreted as one of fascinated admiration.

Presently, when he felt that his audience was about to

grow restive (even though he had to admit that they never would have shown it outwardly) he put on 'Sonny Boy'. From the reaction it was not difficult to guess that this selection was finding less favour with its listeners. The general expression of tense anticipation at the beginning of the record soon relaxed into one of routine enjoyment of a less intense degree. When the piece was finished, Nicolás got to his feet again and raised his hand solemnly, saying: 'Good. But the other music is more beautiful.'

The pastor made a short summation, and, after playing 'Crazy Rhythm' again, he announced that the service was over.

In this way 'Crazy Rhythm' became an integral part of Pastor Dowe's weekly service. After a few months the old record was so badly worn that he determined to play it only once at each gathering. His flock submitted to this show of economy with bad grace. They complained, using Nicolás as emissary.

'But the music is old. There will be no more if I use it all,' the pastor explained.

Nicolás smiled unbelievingly. 'You say that. But you do not want us to have it.'

The following day, as the pastor sat reading in the patio's shade, Mateo again announced Nicolás, who had entered through the kitchen and, it appeared, had been conversing with the servants there. By now the pastor had learned fairly well how to read the expressions on Nicolás's face; the one he saw there now told him that new exactions were at hand.

Nicolás looked respectful. 'Señor,' he said, 'we like you because you have given us music when we asked you for it. Now we are all good friends. We want you to give us salt.'

'Salt?' exclaimed Pastor Dowe, incredulous. 'What for?'

Nicolás laughed good-naturedly, making it clear that he thought the pastor was joking with him. Then he made a gesture of licking. 'To eat,' he said.

'Ah, yes,' murmured the pastor, recalling that among the Indians rock salt is a scarce luxury.

'But we have no salt,' he said quickly.

'Oh, yes, señor. There.' Nicolás indicated the kitchen.

The pastor stood up. He was determined to put an end to

this haggling, which he considered a demoralizing element in his official relationship with the village. Signalling for Nicolás to follow, he walked into the kitchen, calling as he entered, 'Quintina, show me our salt.'

Several of the servants, including Mateo, were standing in the room. It was Mateo who opened a low cupboard and disclosed a great stack of greyish cakes piled on the floor. The pastor was astonished. 'So many kilos of salt!' he exclaimed. '*Cómo se hace?*'

Mateo calmly told him it had been brought with them all the way from Ocosingo. 'For us,' he added, looking about at the others.

Pastor Dowe seized upon this, hoping it was meant as a hint and could be recognized as one. 'Of course,' he said to Nicolás. 'This is for my house.'

Nicolás looked unimpressed. 'You have enough for everyone in the village,' he remarked. 'In two Sundays you can get more from Ocosingo. Everyone will be very happy all the time that way. Everyone will come each time you speak. You give them salt and make music.'

Pastor Dowe felt himself beginning to tremble a little. He knew he was excited and so he was careful to make his voice sound natural.

'I will decide, Nicolás,' he said. 'Goodbye.'

It was clear that Nicolás in no way regarded these words as a dismissal. He answered, 'Goodbye,' and leaned back against the wall calling, 'Marta!' The little girl, of whose presence in the room the pastor now became conscious, moved out from the shadows of a corner. She held what appeared to him to be a large doll, and was being very solicitous of it. As the pastor stepped out into the bright patio, the picture struck him as false, and he turned around and looked back into the kitchen, frowning. He remained in the doorway in an attitude of suspended action for a moment, staring at little Marta. The doll, held lovingly in the child's arms, and swaddled in a much-used rag, was making spasmodic movements.

The pastor's ill humour was with him; probably he would have shown it no matter what the circumstances. 'What is it?' he demanded indignantly. As if in answer the bundle squirmed again, throwing off part of the rag that covered it, and the pastor saw what looked to him like a comic-strip caricature of Red Riding Hood's wolf peering out from under the grandmother's nightcap. Again Pastor Dowe cried, 'What is it?'

Nicolás turned from his conversation, amused, and told Marta to hold it up and uncover it so the señor could see it. This she did, pulling away the wrapping and exposing to view a lively young alligator which, since it was being held more or less on its back, was objecting in a routine fashion to the treatment by rhythmically paddling the air with its little black feet. Its rather long face seemed, however, to be smiling.

'Good heavens!' cried the pastor in English. The spectacle struck him as strangely scandalous. There was a hidden obscenity in the sight of the mildly agitated little reptile with its head wrapped in a rag, but Marta was still holding it out toward him for his inspection. He touched the smooth scales of its belly with his fingers, and withdrew his hand, saying, 'Its jaws should be bound. It will bite her.'

Mateo laughed. 'She is too quick', and then said it in dialect to Nicolás, who agreed, and also laughed. The pastor patted Marta on the head as she returned the animal to her bosom and resumed cradling it tenderly.

Nicolás's eyes were on him. 'You like Marta?' he asked seriously.

The pastor was thinking about the salt. 'Yes, yes,' he said with the false enthusiasm of the preoccupied man. He went to his bedroom and shut the door. Lying on the narrow bed in the afternoon was the same as lying on it at night: there was the same sound of dogs barking in the village. Today there was also the sound of wind going past the window. Even the canopy of mosquito netting swayed a little from time to time as the air came into the room. The pastor was trying to decide whether or not to give in to Nicolás. When he got very sleepy, he thought: After all, what principle am I upholding in keeping it from them? They want music. They want salt. They will learn to want God. This thought proved relaxing to him, and he fell asleep to the sound of the dogs barking and the wind shrilling past the window.

During the night the clouds rolled down off the mountains into the valley, and when dawn came they remained there, impaled on the high trees. The few birds that made themselves heard sounded as though they were singing beneath the ceiling of a great room. The wet air was thick with wood smoke, but there was no noise from the village; a wall of cloud lay between it and the mission house.

From his bed, instead of the wind passing the window, the pastor heard the slow drops of water falling upon the bushes from the eaves. He lay still awhile, lulled by the subdued chatter of the servants' voices in the kitchen. Then he went to the window and looked out into the greyness. Even the nearest trees were invisible; there was a heavy odour of earth. He dressed, shivering as the damp garments touched his skin. On the table lay a newspaper:

BARCELONA BOMBARDEADO POR DOSCIENTOS AVIONES

As he shaved, trying to work up a lather with the tepid water Quintina had brought him, full of charcoal ashes, it occurred to him that he would like to escape from the people of Tacaté and the smothering feeling they gave him of being lost in antiquity. It would be good to be free from that infinite sadness even for a few hours.

He ate a larger breakfast than usual and went outside to the sheltered platform, where he sat down in the dampness and began to read the seventy-eighth psalm, which he had thought of using as the basis of a sermon. As he read he looked out at the emptiness in front of him. Where he knew the mango tree stood he could see only the white void, as if the land dropped away at the platform's edge for a thousand feet or more.

'He clave the rocks in the wilderness, and gave them drink as out of the great depths.' From the house came the sound of Quintina's giggling. Mateo is probably chasing her around the patio, thought the pastor; wisely he had long since given up expecting any Indian to behave as he considered an adult should. Every few seconds on the other side of the pavilion a turkey made its hysterical gobbling sound. The pastor spread his Bible out on the table, put his hands to his ears, and continued to read: 'He caused an east wind to blow in the heaven: and by His power He brought in the south wind.'

Passages like that would sound utterly pagan in the dialect, he caught himself thinking. He unstopped his ears and reflected: But to their ears *everything* must have a pagan sound. Everything I say is transformed on the way to them into something else. This was a manner of thinking that Pastor Dowe had always taken pains to avoid. He fixed his eyes on the text with determination, and read on. The giggling in the house was louder; he could hear Mateo too now. 'He sent divers sorts of flies among them; . . . and frogs, which destroyed them.' The door into the patio was opened and the pastor heard Mateo coughing as he stood looking out. He certainly has tuberculosis, said the pastor to himself, as the Indian spat repeatedly. He shut his Bible and took off his glasses, feeling about on the table for their case. Not encountering it, he rose, and taking a step forward, crushed it under his heel. Compassionately, he stooped down and picked it up. The hinges were snapped and the metal sides under their artificial leather covering were bent out of shape. Mateo could have hammered it back into a semblance of its form, but Pastor Dowe preferred to think: All things have their death. He had had the case eleven years. Briefly he summed up its life: the sunny afternoon when he had bought it on the little side street in downtown Havana; the busy years in the hills of southern Brazil; the time in Chile when he had dropped the case, with a pair of dark glasses in it, out the bus window, and everyone in the bus had got out and helped him look for it; the depressing year in Chicago when for some reason he had left it in a bureau drawer most of the time and had carried his glasses loose in his coat pocket. He remembered some of the newspaper clippings he had kept in the case, and many of the little slips of paper with ideas jotted down on them. He looked tenderly down at it, thinking: And so this is the place and time, and these are the circumstances of its death. For some reason he was happy to have witnessed this death; it was comforting to know exactly how the case had finished its existence. He still looked at it with sadness for a moment. Then he flung it out into the white air as if the precipice were really there. With his Bible under his arm he strode to the door and brushed past Mateo without saying a word. But as he walked into his room it seemed to him that Mateo had looked at him in a strange fashion, as if he knew something and were waiting to see when the pastor would find out, too.

Back in his suffocating little room the pastor felt an even more imperious need to be alone for a time. He changed his shoes, took his cane and went out into the fog. In this weather there was only one path practicable, and that led downward through the village. He stepped ahead over the stones with great caution, for although he could discern the ground at his feet and the spot where he put the tip of his cane each time, beyond that on all sides was mere whiteness. Walking along thus, he reflected, was like trying to read a text with only one letter visible at a time. The wood smoke was sharp in the still air.

For perhaps half an hour Pastor Dowe continued this way, carefully putting one foot before the other. The emptiness around him, the lack of all visual detail, rather than activating his thought, served to dull his perceptions. His progress over the stones was laborious but strangely relaxing. One of the few ideas that came into his head as he moved along was that it would be pleasant to pass through the village without anyone's noticing him, and it seemed to him that it might be managed; even at ten feet he would be invisible. He could walk between the huts and hear the babies crying, and when he came out at the other end no one would know he had been there. He was not sure where he would go then.

The way became suddenly rougher as the path went into a zigzagging descent along the steep side of a ravine. He had reached the bottom before he raised his head once. 'Ah,' he said, standing still. The fog was now above him, a great grey quilt of cloud. He saw the giant trees that stood around him and heard them dripping slowly in a solemn, uneven chorus on to the wild coca leaves beneath.

There is no such place as this on the way to the village, thought the pastor. He was mildly annoyed, but more astonished, to find himself standing by these trees that looked like elephants and were larger than any other trees he had seen in the region. Automatically he turned around in the path and started back up the slope. Beside the overpowering sadness of the landscape, now that it was visible to him, the fog up there was a comfort and a protection. He paused for a moment to stare back at the fat, spiny tree trunks and the welter of vegetation beyond. A small sound behind him made him turn his head.

Two Indians were trotting down the path toward him. As they came up they stopped and looked at him with such expectancy on their dark little faces that Pastor Dowe thought they were going to speak. Instead the one ahead made a grunting sound and motioned to the other to follow. There was no way of effecting a detour around the pastor, so they brushed violently against him as they went by. Without once looking back they hurried on downward and disappeared among the green coca leaves.

This unlikely behaviour on the part of the two natives vaguely intrigued him; on an impulse he determined to find an explanation for it. He started after them.

Soon he had gone beyond the spot where he had turned back a moment ago. He was in the forest; the plant odour was almost unbearable – a smell of living and dead vegetation in a world where slow growth and slow death are simultaneous and inseparable. He stopped once and listened for footsteps. Apparently the Indians had run on ahead of him; nevertheless he continued on his way. Since the path was fairly wide and well broken in, it was only now and then that he came into contact with a hanging tendril or a projecting branch.

The posturing trees and vines gave the impression of having been arrested in furious motion, and presented a monotonous succession of tortured tableaux vivants. It was as if, for the moment while he watched, the desperate battle for air had been suspended and would be resumed only when he turned away his head. As he looked, he decided that it was precisely this unconfirmable quality of surreptitiousness which made the place so disquieting. Now and then, high above his head, a blood-coloured butterfly would float silently through the gloom from one tree trunk to another. They were all alike; it seemed to him that it must be always the same insect. Several times he passed the white grillework of great spider webs flung across between the plants like gates painted on the dark wall behind. But all the webs looked uninhabited. The large, leisurely drops of water still continued to fall from above; even if it had been raining hard, the earth could not have been wetter.

The pastor was astigmatic, and since he was beginning to be dizzy from watching so many details, he kept his eyes looking straight ahead as he walked, deviating his gaze only when he had to avoid the plant life that had grown across the path. The floor of the forest continued flat. Suddenly he became aware that the air around him was reverberating with faint sounds. He stood still, and recognized the casual gurgle a deep stream makes from time to time as it moves past its banks. Almost immediately ahead of him was the water, black and wide, and considering its proximity, incredibly quiet in its swift flowing. A few paces before him a great dead tree, covered with orange fungus, lay across the path. The pastor's glance followed the trunk to the left; at the small end, facing him, sat the two Indians. They were looking at him with interest, and he knew they had been waiting for him. He walked over to them, greeted them. They replied solemnly, never taking their shining eyes from his face. As if they had rehearsed it, they both rose at the same instant and walked to the water's edge, where they stood looking down. Then one of them glanced back at the pastor and said simply, 'Come.' As he made his way around the log he saw that they were standing by a long bamboo raft which was beached on the muddy bank. They one end into the stream.

'Where are you going?' asked the pastor. For reply they lifted their short brown arms in unison and waved them slowly in the direction of downstream. Again the one who had spoken before said, 'Come.' The pastor, his curiosity aroused, looked suspiciously at the delicate raft, and back at the two men. At the same time he felt that it would be pleasanter to be riding with them than to go back through the forest. Impatiently he again demanded, 'Where are you going? Tacaté?'

'Tacaté,' echoed the one who up to this point had not spoken.

'Is it strong?' queried the pastor, stooping to push lightly on a piece of bamboo. This was merely a formality; he had perfect faith in the Indians' ability to master the materials of the jungle.

'Strong,' said the first. 'Come.'

The pastor glanced back into the wet forest, climbed on to the raft, and sat doubled up on its bottom in the stern. The two quickly jumped aboard and pushed the frail craft from the bank with a pole.

Then began a journey which almost at once Pastor Dowe regretted having undertaken. Even as the three of them shot swiftly ahead, around the first bend in the stream, he wished he had stayed behind and could be at this moment on his way up the side of the ravine. And as they sped on down the silent waterway he continued to reproach himself for having come along without knowing why. At each successive bend in the tunnel-like course, he felt further from the world. He found himself straining in a ridiculous effort to hold the raft back: it glided far too easily along the top of the black water. Further from the world, or did he mean further from God? A region like this seemed outside God's jurisdiction. When he had reached that idea he shut his eyes. It was an absurdity, manifestly impossible – in any case, inadmissible – yet it had occurred to him and was remaining with him in his mind. God is always with me, he said to himself silently, but the formula had no effect. He opened his eyes quickly and looked at the two men. They were facing him, but he had the impression of being invisible to them; they could see only the quickly dissipated ripples left behind on the surface of the water, and the irregular arched ceiling of vegetation under which they had passed.

The pastor took his cane from where it was lying hidden, and gesticulated with it as he asked, 'Where are we going?' Once again they both pointed vaguely into the air, over their shoulders, as if the question were of no interest, and the expression on their faces never changed. Loath to let even another tree go past, the pastor mechanically immersed his cane in the water as though he would stop the constant forward thrusting of the raft; he withdrew it immediately and laid it dripping across the bottom. Even that much

contact with the dark stream was unpleasant to him. He tried
to tell himself that there was no reason for his sudden
spiritual collapse, but at the same time it seemed to him that
he could feel the innermost fibres of his consciousness in the
process of relaxing. The journey downstream was a monstrous letting go, and he fought against it with all his power.
'Forgive me, O God, I am leaving you behind. Forgive me
for leaving you behind.' His nails pressed into his palms as he
prayed.

And so he sat in agonized silence while they slid ahead
through the forest and out into a wide lagoon where the grey
sky was once more visible. Here the raft went much more
slowly, and the Indians propelled it gently with their hands
toward the shore where the water was shallow. Then one of
them poled it along with the bamboo stick. The pastor did
not notice the great beds of water hyacinths they passed
through, nor the silken sound they made as they rubbed against
the raft. Out here under the low-hanging clouds there was
occasionally a bird cry or a sudden rustle in the high grass by
the water's edge. Still the pastor remained sunk within
himself, feeling, rather than thinking: Now it is done. I have
passed over into the other land. And he remained so deeply
preoccupied with this emotional certainty that he was not
aware of it when they approached a high escarpment rising
sheer from the lagoon, nor when they drew up on to the sand
of a small cove at one side of the cliff. When he looked up the
two Indians were standing on the sand, and one of them was
saying, 'Come.' They did not help him get ashore; he did this
with some difficulty, although he was conscious of none.

As soon as he was on land they led him along the foot of
the cliff that curved away from the water. Following a
tortuous track beaten through the undergrowth they came
out all at once at the very foot of the wall of rock.

There were two caves – a small one opening to the left, and
a wider, higher one to the right. They halted outside the
smaller. 'Go in,' they said to the pastor. It was not very light
inside, and he could see very little. The two remained at the
entrance. 'Your god lives here,' said one. 'Speak with him.'

The pastor was on his knees. 'O Father, hear my voice. let
my voice come through to you. I ask it in Jesus' name. . . .'

The Indian was calling to him, 'Speak in our tongue.'

The pastor made an effort, and began a halting supplication in the dialect. There were grunts of satisfaction outside. The concentration demanded in order to translate his thoughts into the still unfamiliar language served to clear his mind somewhat. And the comforting parallel between this prayer and those he offered for his congregation helped to restore his calm. As he continued to speak, always with fewer hesitations, he felt a great rush of strength going through him. Confidently he raised his head and went on praying, his eyes on the wall in front of him. At the same moment he heard the cry: 'Metzabok hears you now. Say more to him.'

The pastor's lips stopped moving, and his eyes saw for the first time the red hand painted on the rock before him, and the charcoal, the ashes, the flower petals and the wooden spoons strewn about. But he had no sensation of horror; that was over. The important thing now was that he felt strong and happy. His spiritual condition was a physical fact. Having prayed to Metzabok was also a fact, of course, but his deploring of it was in purely mental terms. Without formulating the thought, he decided that forgiveness would be forthcoming when he asked God for it.

To satisfy the watchers outside the cave he added a few formal phrases to his prayer, rose, and stepped out into the daylight. For the first time he noticed a certain animation in the features of the two little men. One said, 'Metzabok is very happy.' The other said, 'Wait.' Whereupon they both hurried over to the larger of the two apertures and disappeared inside. The pastor sat on a rock, resting his chin on the hand that held the head of his cane. He was still suffused with the strange triumphant sensation of having returned to himself.

He heard them muttering for a quarter of an hour or so inside the cave. Presently they came out, still looking very serious. Moved by curiosity, the pastor risked a question. He indicated the larger cave with a finger and said, 'Hachakyum lives there?' Together they assented. He wanted to go further and ask if Hachakyum approved of his having spoken with Metzabok, but he felt the question would be imprudent;

besides, he was certain the answer would be in the affirmative.

They arrived back in the village at nightfall, after having walked all the way. The Indians' gait had been far too swift for Pastor Dowe, and they had stopped only once to eat some sapotes they had found under the trees. He asked to be taken to the house of Nicolás. It was raining lightly when they reached the hut. The pastor sat down in the doorway beneath the overhanging eaves of cane. He felt utterly exhausted; it had been one of the most tiring days of his life, and he was not home yet.

His two companions ran off when Nicolás appeared. Evidently he already knew of the visit to the cave. It seemed to the pastor that he had never seen his face so full of expression or so pleasant. '*Utz, utz,*' said Nicolás. 'Good, good. You must eat and sleep.'

After a meal of fruit and maize cakes, the pastor felt better. The hut was filled with wood smoke from the fire in the corner. He lay back in a low hammock which little Marta, casually pulling on a string from time to time, kept in gentle motion. He was overcome with a desire to sleep, but his host seemed to be in a communicative mood, and he wanted to profit by it. As he was about to speak, Nicolás approached, carrying a rusty tin biscuit box. Squatting beside the hammock he said in a low voice: 'I will show you my things.' The pastor was delighted; this bespoke a high degree of friendliness. Nicolás opened the box and took out some sample-size squares of printed cloth, an old vial of quinine tablets, a torn strip of newspaper, and four copper coins. He gave the pastor time to examine each carefully. At the bottom of the box were a good many orange and blue feathers which Nicolás did not bother to take out. The pastor realized that he was seeing the treasures of the household, that these items were rare objects of art. He looked at each thing with great seriousness handing it back with a verbal expression of admiration. Finally he said: 'Thank you', and fell back into the hammock. Nicolás returned the box to the women sitting in the corner. When he came back over to the pastor he said: 'Now we sleep.'

'Nicolás,' asked the pastor, 'is Metzabok bad?'

'*Bai*, señor. Sometimes very bad. Like a small child. When he does not get what he wants right away, he makes fires, fever, wars. He can be very good, too, when he is happy. You should speak with him every day. Then you will know him.'

'But you never speak with him.'

'*Bai*, we do. Many do, when they are sick or unhappy. They ask him to take away the trouble. I never speak with him,' Nicolás looked pleased, 'because Hachakyum is my good friend and I do not need Metzabok. Besides, Metzabok's home is far – three hours' walk. I can speak with Hachakyum here.' The pastor knew he meant the little altar outside. He nodded and fell asleep.

The village in the early morning was a chaos of shrill sounds: dogs, parrots and cockatoos, babies, turkeys. The pastor lay still in his hammock awhile listening, before he was officially wakened by Nicolás. 'We must go now, señor,' he said. 'Everyone is waiting for you.'

The pastor sat up, a little bit alarmed. 'Where?' he cried.

'You speak and make music today.'

'Yes, yes.' He had quite forgotten it was Sunday.

The pastor was silent, walking beside Nicolás up the road to the mission. The weather had changed, and the early sun was very bright. I have been fortified by my experience, he was thinking. His head was clear; he felt amazingly healthy. The unaccustomed sensation of vigour gave him a strange nostalgia for the days of his youth. I must always have felt like this then. I remember it, he thought.

At the mission there was a great crowd – many more people than he had ever seen attend a sermon at Tacaté. They were chatting quietly, but when he and Nicolás appeared there was an immediate hush. Mateo was standing in the pavilion waiting for him, with the phonograph open. With a pang the pastor realized he had not prepared a sermon for his flock. He went into the house for a moment, and returned to seat himself at the table in the pavilion, where he picked up his Bible. He had left his few notes in the book, so that it opened to the seventy-eighth psalm. I shall read them that, he decided. He turned to Mateo. 'Play the *disco*,' he said. Mateo put on 'Crazy Rhythm'. The pastor quickly made a few pencil alterations in the text of the psalm, substituting the names of minor local deities, like Usukun and Sibanaa for such names as Jacob and Ephraim, and local place names for Israel and Egypt. And he wrote the word Hachakyum each time the word God or the Lord appeared. He had not finished when the record stopped. 'Play it again,' he commanded. The audience was delighted, even though the sound was abominably scratchy. When the music was over for the second time, he stood and began to paraphrase the psalm in a clear voice. 'The children of Sibanaa, carrying bows to shoot, ran into the forest to hide when the enemy came. They did not keep their promises to Hachakyum, and they would not live as he told them to live.' The audience was electrified. As he spoke, he looked down and saw the child Marta staring up at him. She had let go of her baby alligator, and it was crawling with a surprising speed toward the table where he sat. Quintina, Mateo, and the two maids were piling up the bars of salt on the ground to one side. They kept returning to the kitchen for more. He realized that what he was saying doubtless made no sense in terms of his listeners' religion, but it was a story of the unleashing of divine displeasure upon an unholy people, and they were enjoying it vastly. The alligator, trailing its rags, had crawled to within a few inches of the pastor's feet, where it remained quiet, content to be out of Marta's arms.

Presently, while he was still speaking, Mateo began to hand out the salt, and soon they all were running their tongues rhythmically over the large rough cakes, but continuing to pay strict attention to his words. When he was about to finish, he motioned to Mateo to be ready to start the record again the minute he finished; on the last word he lowered his arm as a signal, and 'Crazy Rhythm' sounded once more. The alligator began to crawl hastily toward the far end of the pavilion. Pastor Dowe bent down and picked it up. As he stepped forward to hand it to Mateo, Nicolás rose from the ground, and taking Marta by the hand, walked over into the pavilion with her.

'Señor,' he said, 'Marta will live with you. I give her to you.'

'What do you mean?' cried the pastor in a voice which

cracked a little. The alligator squirmed in his hand.

'She is your wife. She will live here.'

Pastor Dowe's eyes grew very wide. He was unable to say anything for a moment. He shook his hands in the air and finally he said: 'No' several times.

Nicolás's face grew unpleasant. 'You do not like Marta?'

'Very much. She is beautiful.' The pastor sat down slowly on his chair. 'But she is a little child.'

Nicolás frowned with impatience. 'She is already large.'

'No, Nicolás. No. No.'

Nicolás pushed his daughter forward and stepped back several paces, leaving her there by the table. 'It is done,' he said sternly. 'She is your wife. I have given her to you.'

Pastor Dowe looked out over the assembly and saw the unspoken approval in all the faces. 'Crazy Rhythm' ceased to play. There was silence. Under the mango tree he saw a woman toying with a small, shiny object. Suddenly he recognized his glasses case; the woman was stripping the leatheroid fabric from it. The bare aluminium with its dents flashed in the sun. For some reason even in the middle of this situation he found himself thinking: So I was wrong. It is not dead. She will keep it, the way Nicolás has kept the quinine tablets.

He looked down at Marta. The child was staring at him quite without expression. Like a cat, he reflected.

Again he began to protest. 'Nicolás,' he cried, his voice very high, 'this is impossible!' He felt a hand grip his arm, and turned to receive a warning glance from Mateo.

Nicolás had already advanced toward the pavilion, his face like a thundercloud. As he seemed about to speak, the pastor interrupted him quickly. He had decided to temporize. 'She may stay at the mission today,' he said weakly.

'She is your wife,' said Nicolás with great feeling. 'You cannot send her away. You must keep her.'

'*Diga que si*,' Mateo was whispering. 'Say yes, señor.'

'Yes,' the pastor heard himself saying. 'Yes. Good.' He got up and walked slowly into the house, holding the alligator with one hand and pushing Marta in front of him with the other. Mateo followed and closed the door after them.

'Take her into the kitchen, Mateo,' said the pastor dully,

handing the little reptile to Marta. As Mateo went across the patio leading the child by the hand, he called after him. 'Leave her with Quintina and come to my room.'

He sat down on the edge of his bed, staring ahead of him with unseeing eyes. At each moment his predicament seemed to him more terrible. With relief he heard Mateo knock. The people outdoors were slowly leaving. It cost him an effort to call out, '*Adelante*.' When Mateo had come in, the pastor said, 'Close the door.'

'Mateo, did you know they were going to do this? That they were going to bring that child here?'

'*Sí, señor.*'

'You knew it! But why didn't you say anything? Why didn't you tell me?'

Mateo shrugged his shoulders, looking at the floor. 'I didn't know it would matter to you,' he said. 'Anyway, it would have been useless.'

'Useless? Why? You could have stopped Nicolás,' said the pastor, although he did not believe it himself.

Mateo laughed shortly. 'You think so?'

'Mateo, you must help me. We must oblige Nicolás to take her back.'

Mateo shook his head. 'It can't be done. These people are very severe. They never change their laws.'

'Perhaps a letter to the administrator at Ocosingo . . .'

'No, señor. That would make still more trouble. You are not a Catholic.' Mateo shifted on his feet and suddenly smiled thinly. 'Why not let her stay? She doesn't eat much. She can work in the kitchen. In two years she will be very pretty.'

The pastor jumped, and made such a wide and vehement gesture with his hands that the mosquito netting, looped above his head, fell down about this face. Mateo helped him disentangle himself. The air smelled of dust from the netting.

'You don't understand anything!' shouted Pastor Dowe, beside himself. 'I can't talk to you! I don't want to talk to you! Go out and leave me alone.' Mateo obediently left the room.

Pounding his left palm with his right fist, over and over again, the pastor stood in his window before the landscape that shone in the strong sun. A few women were still eating under the mango tree; the rest had gone back down the hill.

He lay on his bed throughout the long afternoon. When twilight came he had made his decision. Locking his door, he proceeded to pack what personal effects he could into his smallest suitcase. His Bible and notebooks went on top with his toothbrush and atabrine tablets. When Quintina came to announce supper he asked to have it brought to his bed, taking care to slip the packed valise into the closet before he unlocked the door for her to enter. He waited until the talking had ceased all over the house, until he knew everyone was asleep. With the small bag not too heavy in one hand he tiptoed into the patio, out through the door into the fragrant night, across the open space in front of the pavilion, under the mango tree and down the path leading to Tacaté. Then he began to walk fast, because he wanted to get through the village before the moon rose.

There was a chorus of dogs barking as he entered the village street. He began to run, straight through to the other end. And he kept running even then, until he had reached the point where the path, wider here, dipped beneath the hill and curved into the forest. His heart was beating rapidly from the exertion. To rest, and to try to be fairly certain he was not being followed, he sat down on his little valise in the centre of the path. There he remained a long time, thinking of nothing, while the night went on and the moon came up. He heard only the light wind among the leaves and vines. Overhead a few bats reeled soundlessly back and forth. At last he took a deep breath, got up, and went on.

The Circular Valley

The abandoned monastery stood on a slight eminence of land in the middle of a vast clearing. On all sides the ground sloped gently downward toward the tangled, hairy jungle that filled the circular valley, ringed about by sheer, black cliffs. There were a few trees in some of the courtyards, and the birds used them as meeting-places when they flew out of the rooms and corridors where they had their nests. Long ago bandits had taken whatever was removable out of the building. Soldiers had used it once as headquarters, had, like the bandits, built fires in the great windy rooms so that afterward they looked like ancient kitchens. And now that everything was gone from within, it seemed that never again would anyone come near the monastery. The vegetation had thrown up a protecting wall; the first storey was soon quite hidden from view by small trees which dripped vines to lasso the cornices of the windows. The meadows round about grew dank and lush; there was no path through them.

At the higher end of the circular valley a river fell off the cliffs into a great cauldron of vapour and thunder below; after this it slid along the base of the cliffs until it found a gap at the other end of the valley, where it hurried discreetly through with no rapids, no cascades – a great thick black rope of water moving swiftly downhill between the polished flanks of the canyon. Beyond the gap the land opened out and became smiling; a village nestled on the hillside just outside. In the days of the monastery it was there that the friars had got their provisions, since the Indians would not enter the circular valley. Centuries ago when the building had been constructed the Church had imported the workmen from another part of the country. These were traditional enemies of the tribes thereabouts, and had another language; there was no danger that the inhabitants would communicate with them as they worked at setting up the mighty walls. Indeed, the construction had taken so long that before the east wing was completed the workmen had all died, one by one. Thus it was the friars themselves who had closed off the end of the wing with blank walls, leaving it that way, unfinished and blind-looking, facing the black cliffs.

Generation after generation, the friars came, fresh-cheeked boys who grew thin and grey, and finally died, to be buried in the garden beyond the courtyard with the fountain. One day not long ago they had all left the monastery; no one knew where they had gone, and no one thought to ask. It was shortly after this that the bandits, and then the soldiers had come. And now, since the Indians do not change, still no one from the village went up through the gap to visit the monastery. The Atlájala lived there; the friars had not been able to kill it, had given up at last and gone away. No one was surprised, but the Atlájala gained in prestige by their departure. During the centuries the friars had been there in the monastery, the Indians had wondered why it allowed them to stay. Now, at last, it had driven them out. It always had lived there, they said, and would go on living there because the valley was its home, and it could never leave.

In the early morning the restless Atlájala would move through the halls of the monastery. The dark rooms sped past, one after the other. In a small patio, where eager young trees had pushed up the paving stones to reach the sun, it paused. The air was full of small sounds: the movements of butterflies, the falling to the ground of bits of leaves and flowers, the air following its myriad courses around the edges of things, the ants pursuing their endless labours in the hot dust. In the sun it waited, conscious of each gradation in sound and light and smell, living in the awareness of the slow, constant disintegration that attacked the morning and transformed it into afternoon. When evening came, it often slipped above the monastery roof and surveyed the darkening sky: the waterfall would roar distantly. Night after night, along the procession of years, it had hovered here above the valley, darting down to become a bat, a leopard, a moth for a few minutes or hours, returning to rest immobile in the centre of the space enclosed by the cliffs. When the monastery had been built, it had taken to frequenting the rooms, where it had observed for the first time the meaningless gestures of human life.

And then one evening it had aimlessly become one of the young friars. This was a new sensation, strangely rich and complex, and at the same time unbearably stifling, as though every other possibility besides that of being enclosed in a tiny, isolated world of cause and effect had been removed for ever. As the friar, it had gone and stood in the window, looking out at the sky, seeing for the first time, not the stars, but the space between and beyond them. Even at that moment it had felt the urge to leave, to step outside the little shell of anguish where it lodged for the moment, but a faint curiosity had impelled it to remain a little longer and partake a little further of the unaccustomed sensation. It held on; the friar raised his arms to the sky in an imploring gesture. For the first time the Atlájala sensed opposition, the thrill of a struggle. It was delicious to feel the young man striving to free himself of its presence, and it was immeasurably sweet to remain there. Then with a cry the friar had rushed to the other side of the room and seized a heavy leather whip hanging on the wall. Tearing off his clothing he had begun to carry out a ferocious self-beating. At the first blow of the lash the Atlájala had been on the point of letting go, but then it realized that the immediacy of that intriguing inner pain was only made more manifest by the impact of the blows from without, and so it stayed and felt the young man grow weak under his own lashing. When he had finished and said a prayer, he crawled to his pallet and fell asleep weeping, while the Atlájala slipped out obliquely and entered into a bird which passed the night sitting in a great tree on the edge of the jungle, listening intently to the night sounds, and uttering a scream from time to time.

Thereafter the Atlájala found it impossible to resist sliding inside the bodies of the friars; it visited one after the other, finding an astonishing variety of sensation in the process.

Each was a separate world, a separate experience, because each had different reactions when he became conscious of the other being within him. One would sit and read or pray, one would go for a long troubled walk in the meadows, around and around the building, one would find a comrade and engage in an absurd but bitter quarrel, a few wept, some flagellated themselves or sought a friend to wield the lash for them. Always there was a rich profusion of perceptions for the Atlájala to enjoy, so that it no longer occurred to it to frequent the bodies of insects, birds and furred animals, nor even to leave the monastery and move in the air above. Once it almost got into difficulties when an old friar it was occupying suddenly fell back dead. That was a hazard it ran in the frequenting of men: they seemed not to know when they were doomed, or if they did know, they pretended with such strength not to know, that it amounted to the same thing. The other beings knew beforehand, save when it was a question of being seized unawares and devoured. And that the Atlájala was able to prevent: a bird in which it was staying was always avoided by the hawks and eagles.

When the friars left the monastery, and, following the government's orders, doffed their robes, dispersed and became workmen, the Atlájala was at a loss to know how to pass its days and nights. Now everything was as it had been before their arrival: there was no one but the creatures that always had lived in the circular valley. It tried a giant serpent, a deer, a bee: nothing had the savour it had grown to love. Everything was the same as before, but not for the Atlájala; it had known the existence of man, and now there were no men in the valley – only the abandoned building with its empty rooms to make man's absence more poignant.

Then one year bandits came, several hundred of them in one stormy afternoon. In delight it tried many of them as they sprawled about cleaning their guns and cursing, and it discovered still other facets of sensation: the hatred they felt for the world, the fear they had of the soldiers who were pursuing them, the strange gusts of desire that swept through them as they sprawled together drunk by the fire that smouldered in the centre of the floor, and the insufferable pain of jealousy which the nightly orgies seemed to awaken in some of them. But the bandits did not stay long. When they had left, the soldiers came in their wake. It felt very much the same way to be a soldier as to be a bandit. Missing were the strong fear and the hatred, but the rest was almost identical. Neither the bandits nor the soldiers appeared to be at all conscious of its presence in them; it could slip from one man to another without causing any change in their behaviour. This surprised it, since its effect on the friars had been so definite, and it felt a certain disappointment at the impossibility of making its existence known to them.

Nevertheless, the Atlájala enjoyed both bandits and soldiers immensely, and was even more desolate when it was left alone once again. It would become one of the swallows that made their nests in the rocks beside the top of the waterfall. In the burning sunlight it would plunge again and again into the curtain of mist that rose from far below, sometimes uttering exultant cries. It would spend a day as a plant louse, crawling slowly along the under side of the leaves, living quietly in the huge green world down there which is for ever hidden from the sky. Or at night, in the velvet body of a panther, it would know the pleasure of the kill. Once for a year it lived in an eel at the bottom of the pool below the waterfall, feeling the mud give slowly before it as it pushed ahead with its flat nose; that was a restful period, but afterward the desire to know again the mysterious life of man had returned – an obsession of which it was useless to try to rid itself. And now it moved restlessly through the ruined rooms, a mute presence, alone, and thirsting to be incarnate once again, but in man's flesh only. And with the building of highways through the country it was inevitable that people should come once again to the circular valley.

A man and a woman drove their automobile as far as a village down in a lower valley; hearing about the ruined monastery and the waterfall that dropped over the cliffs into the great amphitheatre, they determined to see these things. They came on burros as far as the village outside the gap, but there the Indians they had hired to accompany them refused to go any further, and so they continued alone, upward through the canyon and into the precinct of the Atlájala.

It was noon when they rode into the valley; the black ribs

of the cliffs glistened like glass in the sun's blistering downward rays. They stopped the burros by a cluster of boulders at the edge of the sloping meadows. The man got down first, and reached up to help the woman off. She leaned forward, putting her hands on his face, and for a long moment they kissed. Then he lifted her to the ground and they climbed hand in hand up over the rocks. The Atlájala hovered near them, watching the woman closely: she was the first ever to have come into the valley. The two sat beneath a small tree on the grass, looking at one another, smiling. Out of habit, the Atlájala entered into the man. Immediately, instead of existing in the midst of the sunlit air, the bird calls and the plant odours, it was conscious only of the woman's beauty and her terrible imminence. The waterfall, the earth, and the sky itself receded, rushed into nothingness, and there were only the woman's smile and her arms and her odour. It was a world more suffocating and painful than the Atlájala had thought possible. Still, while the man spoke and the woman answered, it remained within.

'Leave him. He doesn't love you.'

'He would kill me.'

'But I love you. I need you with me.'

'I can't. I'm afraid of him.'

The man reached out to pull her to him; she drew back slightly, but her eyes grew large.

'We have today,' she murmured, turning her face toward the yellow walls of the monastery.

The man embraced her fiercely, crushing her against him as though the act would save his life. 'No, no, no. It can't go on like this,' he said. 'No.'

The pain of his suffering was too intense; gently the Atlájala left the man and slipped into the woman. And now it would have believed itself to be housed in nothing, to be in its own spaceless self, so completely was it aware of the wandering wind, the small flutterings of the leaves, and the bright air that surrounded it. Yet there was a difference: each element was magnified in intensity, the whole sphere of being was immense, limitless. Now it understood what the man sought in the woman, and it knew that he suffered because he never would attain that sense of completion he sought. But the Atlájala, being one with the woman, had attained it, and being aware of possessing it, trembled with delight. The woman shuddered as her lips met those of the man. There on the grass in the shade of the tree their joy reached new heights; the Atlájala, knowing them both, formed a single channel between the secret springs of their desires. Throughout, it remained within the woman, and began vaguely to devise ways of keeping her, if not inside the valley, at least near by, so that she might return.

In the afternoon, with dreamlike motions, they walked to the burros and mounted them, driving them through the deep meadow grass to the monastery. Inside the great courtyard they halted, looking hesitantly at the ancient arches in the sunlight, and at the darkness inside the doorways.

'Shall we go in?' said the woman.

'We must get back.'

'I want to go in,' she said. (The Atlájala exulted.) A thin grey snake slid along the ground into the bushes. They did not see it.

The man looked at her perplexedly. 'It's late,' he said.

But she jumped down from her burro by herself and walked beneath the arches into the long corridor within. (Never had the rooms seemed so real as now when the Atlájala was seeing them through her eyes.)

They explored all the rooms. Then the woman wanted to climb up into the tower, but the man took a determined stand.

'We must go back now,' he said firmly, putting his hand on her shoulder.

'This is our only day together, and you think of nothing but getting back.'

'But the time . . .'

'There is a moon. We won't lose the way.'

He would not change his mind. 'No.'

'As you like,' she said. 'I'm going up. You can go back alone if you like.'

The man laughed uneasily. 'You're mad.' He tried to kiss her.

She turned away and did not answer for a moment. Then she said: 'You want me to leave my husband for you. You ask everything from me, but what do you do for me in return? You refuse even to climb up into a little tower with me to see the view. Go back alone. Go!'

She sobbed and rushed toward the dark stairwell. Calling after her, he followed, but stumbled somewhere behind her. She was as sure of foot as if she had climbed the many stone steps a thousand times before, hurrying up through the darkness, around and around.

In the end she came out at the top and peered through the small apertures in the cracking walls. The beams which had supported the bell had rotted and fallen; the heavy bell lay on its side in the rubble, like a dead animal. The waterfall's sound was louder up here; the valley was nearly full of shadow. Below, the man called her name repeatedly. She did not answer. As she stood watching the shadow of the cliffs slowly overtake the furthest recesses of the valley and begin to climb the naked rocks to the east, an idea formed in her mind. It was not the kind of idea which she would have expected of herself, but it was there, growing and inescapable. When she felt it complete there inside her, she turned and went lightly back down. The man was sitting in the dark near the bottom of the stairs, groaning a little.

'What is it?' she said.

'I hurt my leg. Now are you ready to go or not?'

'Yes,' she said simply. 'I'm sorry you fell.'

Without saying anything he rose and limped after her out into the courtyard where the burros stood. The cold mountain air was beginning to flow down from the tops of the cliffs. As they rode through the meadow she began to think of how she would broach the subject to him. (It must be done before they reached the gap. The Atlájala trembled.)

'Do you forgive me?' she asked him.

'Of course,' he laughed.

'Do you love me?'

'More than anything in the world.'

'Is that true?'

He glanced at her in the failing light, sitting erect on the jogging animal. 'You know it is,' he said softly.

She hesitated. 'There is only one way, then,' she said finally.

'But what?'

'I'm afraid of him. I won't go back to him. You go back. I'll stay in the village here.' (Being that near, she would come each day to the monastery.) 'When it is done, you will come and get me. Then we can go somewhere else. No one will find us.'

The man's voice sounded strange. 'I don't understand.'

'You do understand. And that is the only way. Do it or not, as you like. It is the only way.'

They trotted along for a while in silence. The canyon loomed ahead, black against the evening sky.

Then the man said, very clearly: 'Never.'

A moment later the trail led out into an open space high above the swift water below. The hollow sound of the river reached them faintly. The light in the sky was almost gone; in the dusk the landscape had taken on false contours. Everything was grey – the rocks, the bushes, the trail – and nothing had distance or scale. They slowed their pace.

His word still echoed in her ears.

'I won't go back to him!' she cried with sudden vehemence. 'You can go back and play cards with him as usual. Be his good friend the same as always. I won't go. I can't go on with both of you in the town.' (The plan was not working; the Atlájala saw it had lost her, yet it still could help her.)

'You're very tired,' he said softly.

He was right. Almost as he said the words, that unaccustomed exhilaration and lightness she had felt ever since noon seemed to leave her; she hung her head wearily, and said: 'Yes, I am.'

At the same moment the man uttered a sharp, terrible cry; she looked up in time to see his burro plunge from the edge of the trail into the greyness below. There was a silence, and then the far-away sound of many stones sliding downward. She could not move or stop the burro; she sat dumbly, letting it carry her along, an inert weight on its back.

For one final instant, as she reached the pass which was the edge of its realm, the Atlájala alighted tremulously within her. She raised her head and a tiny exultant shiver passed through her; then she let it fall forward once again.

Hanging in the dim air above the trail, the Atlájala watched her indistinct figure grow invisible in the gathering night. (If it had not been able to hold her there, still it had been able to help her.)

A moment later it was in the tower, listening to the spiders mend the webs that she had damaged. It would be a long, long time before it would bestir itself to enter into another being's awareness. A long, long time – perhaps for ever.

The Scorpion

An old woman lived in a cave which her sons had hollowed out of a clay cliff near a spring before they went away to the town where many people live. She was neither happy nor unhappy to be there, because she knew that the end of life was near and that her sons would not be likely to return no matter what the season. In the town there are always many things to do, and they would be doing them, not caring to remember the time when they had lived in the hills looking after the old woman.

At the entrance to the cave at certain times of the year there was a curtain of water drops through which the old woman had to pass to get inside. The water rolled down the bank from the plants above and dripped on to the clay below. So the old woman accustomed herself to sitting crouched in the cave for long periods of time in order to keep as dry as possible. Outside through the moving beads of water she saw the bare earth lighted by the grey sky, and sometimes large dry leaves went past, pushed by the wind that came from higher parts of the land. Inside where she was the light was pleasant and of a pink colour from the clay all around.

A few people used to pass from time to time along the path not far away, and because there was a spring near by, those travellers who knew that it existed but not just where it was would sometimes come near to the cave before they discovered that the spring was not there. The old woman would never call to them. She would merely watch them as they came near and suddenly saw her. Then she would go on watching as they turned back and went in other directions looking for the water to drink.

102

There were many things about this life that the old woman liked. She was no longer obliged to argue and fight with her sons to make them carry wood to the charcoal oven. She was free to move about at night and look for food. She could eat everything she found without having to share it. And she owed no one any debt of thanks for the things she had in her life.

One old man used to come from the village on his way down to the valley, and sit on a rock just distant enough from the cave for her to recognize him. She knew he was aware of her presence in the cave there, and although she probably did not know this, she disliked him for not giving some sign that he knew she was there. It seemed to her that he had an unfair advantage over her and was using it in an unpleasant way. She thought up many ideas for annoying him if he should ever come near enough, but he always passed by in the distance, pausing to sit down on the rock for some time, when he would often gaze straight at the cave. Then he would continue slowly on his way, and it always seemed to the old woman that he went more slowly after his rest than before it.

There were scorpions in the cave all year round, but above all during the days just before the plants began to let water drip through. The old woman had a huge bundle of rags, and with this she would brush the walls and ceiling clear of them, stamping quickly on them with her hard bare heel. Occasionally a small wild bird or animal strayed inside the entrance, but she was never quick enough to kill it, and she had given up trying.

One dark day she looked up to see one of her sons standing in the doorway. She could not remember which one it was, but she thought it was the one who had ridden the horse down the dry river bed and nearly been killed. She looked at his hand to see if it was out of shape. It was not that son.

He began to speak: 'Is it you?'

'Yes.'

'Are you well?'

'Yes.'

'Is everything well?'

'Everything.'

'You stayed here?'

'You can see.'

'Yes.'

There was a silence. The old woman looked around the cave and was displeased to see that the man in the doorway made it practically dark in there. She busied herself with trying to distinguish various objects: her stick, her gourd, her tin can, her length of rope. She was frowning with the effort.

The man was speaking again.

'Shall I come in?'

She did not reply.

He backed away from the entrance, brushing the water drops from his garments. He was on the point of saying something profane, thought the old woman, who, even though she did not know which one this was, remembered what he would do.

She decided to speak.

'What?' she said.

He leaned forward through the curtain of water and repeated his question.

'Shall I come in?'

'No.'

'What's the matter with you?'

'Nothing.'

Then she added: 'There's no room.'

He backed out again, wiping his head. The old woman thought he would probably go away, and she was not sure she wanted him to. However, there was nothing else he could do, she thought. She heard him sit down outside the cave, and then she smelled tobacco smoke. There was no sound but the dripping of water upon the clay.

A short while later she heard him get up. He stood outside the entrance again.

'I'm coming in,' he said.

She did not reply.

He bent over and pushed inside. The cave was too low for him to stand up in it. He looked about and spat on the floor.

'Come on,' he said.

'Where?'

'With me.'

'Why?'

'Because you have to come.'

She waited a little while, and then said suspiciously: 'Where are you going?'

He pointed indifferently toward the valley, and said: 'Down that way.'

'In the town?'

'Further.'

'I won't go.'

'You have to come.'

'No.'

He picked up her stick and held it out to her.

'Tomorrow,' she said.

'Now.'

'I must sleep,' she said, settling back into her pile of rags.

'Good. I'll wait outside,' he answered, and went out.

The old woman went to sleep immediately. She dreamed that the town was very large. It went on for ever and its streets were filled with people in new clothes. The church had a high tower with several bells that rang all the time. She was in the streets all one day, surrounded by people. She was not sure whether they were all her sons or not. She asked some of them: 'Are you my sons?' They could not answer, but she thought that if they had been able to, they would have said: 'Yes.' Then when it was night she found a house with its door open. Inside there was a light and some women were seated in a corner. They rose when she went in, and said: 'You have a room here.' She did not want to see it, but they pushed her along until she was in it, and closed the door. She was a little girl and she was crying. The bells of the church were very loud outside, and she imagined they filled the sky. There was an open space in the wall high above her. She could see the stars through it, and they gave light to her room. From the reeds which formed the ceiling a scorpion came crawling. He came slowly down the wall toward her. She stopped crying and watched him. His tail curved up over his back and moved a little from side to side as he crawled. She looked quickly about for something to brush him down with. Since there was nothing in the room she used her hand. But her motions were slow, and the scorpion seized her finger with his pinchers, clinging there tightly although she waved her hand wildly about. Then she realized that he was not going to sting her. A great feeling of happiness went through her. She raised her finger to her lips to kiss the scorpion. The bells stopped ringing. Slowly in the peace which was beginning, the scorpion moved into her mouth. She felt his hard shell and his little clinging legs going across her lips and her tongue. He crawled slowly down her throat and was hers. She woke up and called out.

Her son answered: 'What is it?'

'I'm ready.'

'So soon?'

He stood outside as she came through the curtain of water, leaning on her stick. Then he began walking a few paces ahead of her toward the path.

'It will rain,' said her son.

'Is it far?'

'Three days,' he said, looking at her old legs.

She nodded. Then she noticed the old man sitting on the stone. He had an expression of deep surprise on his face, as if a miracle had just occurred. His mouth was open as he stared at the old woman. When they came opposite the rock he peered more intently than ever into her face. She pretended not to notice him. As they picked their way carefully downhill along the stony path, they heard the old man's thin voice behind them, carried by the wind.

'Goodbye.'

'Who is that?' said her son.

'I don't know.'

Her son looked back at her darkly.

'You're lying,' he said.

Señor Ong and Señor Ha

At the end of the town's long street a raw green mountain cut across the sky at a forty-five-degree angle, its straight slope moving violently from the cloudy heights down into the valley where the river ran. In the valley, although the land was fertile, there were no farms or orchards, because the people of the town were lazy and did not want to bother clearing away the rocks that strewed the ground. And then, it was always too hot for that sort of work, and everybody had malaria there, so that long ago the town had fallen into its little pattern of living off the Indians who came down from the mountains with food and went back with cheap cloth, machetes and things like mirrors or empty bottles. Life always had been easy; although no one in the town was rich, still, no one ever went hungry. Almost every house had some papayas and a mango tree beside it, and there were plenty of avocados and pineapples to be had in the market for next to nothing.

Some of this had changed when the government had begun the building of the great dam up above. No one seemed to know exactly where the dam was; they were building it somewhere up in the mountains; already the water had covered several villages, and now after six years the construction was still going on. This last was the important part, because it meant that when the Indians came down from above they now brought with them not only food but money. Thus it had come about that certain people in the town had suddenly found themselves rich. They could scarcely believe it themselves, but there was the money, and still the Indians went on coming down and leaving more and more of it on the counters of their shops. They did not know what to do with all these unexpected pesos. Most of them bought huge radios which they kept going from early morning until night, all tuned in full strength to Tapachula, so that when they walked the length of the main street they were never out of earshot of the programme and could follow it without a break. But still they had money. Pepe Jimenez had bought a bright new automobile in the capital, but by the time he had arrived back in town with it, after driving it over the sixty miles of trail from Mapastenango, it was no longer an object to excite admiration, and he felt that he had made an unwise purchase. Even the main street was too bumpy and muddy for him to drive it up and down, and so it stood rusting in front of Mi Esperanza, the bar by the bridge. When they came out of school Nicho and his companions would play in it, pretending it was a fort. But then a group of larger boys from the upper end of the town had come one day and appropriated the car for their own games, so that the boys who lived by the river no longer dared to approach it.

Nicho lived with his aunt in a small house whose garden ended in a wilderness of plants and vines; just below them rushed the river, dashing sideways from boulder to boulder in its shallow mist-filled canyon. The house was clean and simple, and they lived quietly. Nicho's aunt was a woman of too easygoing a nature. Being conscious of this, she felt that one way of giving her dead sister's child the proper care was to attempt to instil discipline in him; the discipline consisted in calling him by his true name, which was Dionisio.

Nor did she have any conception of discipline as far as her own living was concerned, so that the boy was not astonished when the day came that she said to him: 'Dionisio, you will have to stop going to school. We have no more money. Don Anastasio will hire you at ten pesos a month to work in his store, and you can get the noonday meal there too. *Lástima*, but there is no money!'

For a week Nicho sat in the shop learning the prices of the articles that Don Anastasio sold, and then one evening when he went home he found a strange-looking man in the house, sitting in the other rocking-chair opposite his aunt. The man looked a little like some of the Indians that came down from the furthest and highest mountains, but his skin was lighter, he was plumper and softer-seeming, and his eyes were almost shut. He smiled at the boy, but not in a way that Nicho thought very friendly, and shook hands without getting up from his chair. That night his aunt looked really quite happy, and as they were getting ready for bed she said to him: 'Señor Ong is coming to live with us. You will not have to work any more. God has been good to us.'

But it occurred to Nicho that if Señor Ong was to live with them, he would prefer to go on working at Don Anastasio's, in order not to be around the house and so have to see Señor Ong so much. Tactfully, he said: 'I like Don Anastasio.' His aunt looked at him sharply. 'Señor Ong does not want you to work. He is a proud man, and rich enough to feed us both. It is nothing for him. He showed me his money.'

Nicho was not at all pleased, and he went to sleep slowly, his mind full of misgivings. He was afraid that one day he would fight with Señor Ong. And besides, what would his friends say? Señor Ong was such a strange-looking man. But the very next morning he arrived from the Hotel Paraiso with three boys whom Nicho knew, and each boy carried a large bag on his head. From the garden he watched them accept the generous tips Señor Ong gave them and then run off to school without waiting to see whether Nicho wanted to speak to them or not. 'Very bad,' he said to himself as he kicked a stone around and around the bare earth floor of the garden. A little while later he went down to the river and sat on top of the highest boulder watching the milky water that churned beneath him. One of his five cockatoos was screaming from the tangle of leaves on the banks. *'Callate!'* he yelled at it; his own ill humour annoyed him as much as Señor Ong's arrival.

And everything turned out much as he had feared – only worse. Two days later, one of the boys from the upper end of the street said to him in passing: *'Hola, Chale!'* He replied to the greeting automatically and walked on, but a second later he said to himself: *Chale?* But that means Chinaman! Chink! Of course. Señor Ong must be a Chinaman. He turned to look at the boy, and thought of hitting him in the back with a stone. Then he hung his head and walked on slowly. Nothing would do any good.

Little by little the joke spread, and soon even his own friends called him *Chale* when they met him, and although it was really he who had become less friendly, he imagined that they all were avoiding him, that no one wanted to see him any more, and he spent most of his time playing by the river. The water's sound was deafening, but at the same time it made him feel a little bit better.

Neither Señor Ong nor his aunt paid much attention to him, save for their constant mealtime demands that he eat. 'Now that we have more food than we need, you don't want to eat it,' said his aunt angrily. 'Eat, Dionisio,' smiled Señor Ong, '*Bien*,' said Nicho, full of resentment, but in a tone of mock resignation, and pulled off a small piece of tortilla which he chewed very slowly.

There seemed to be no question of his returning to school; at least, the subject was never mentioned, for which he was most grateful, since he had no desire to be back in the midst of his friends just to hear them call him *Chale*. The name by itself would have been bearable if only it had not implied the ridicule of his home life; his powerlessness to change that condition seemed much more shameful than any state of affairs for which he himself might have been at fault. And so he spent his days down by the river, jumping like a goat across the rocks, throwing stones to frighten the vultures away from the carcasses the water left for them, finding deep pools to swim in, and following the river downstream to lie idly naked on the rocks in the hot sun. No matter how pleasant to him Señor Ong might be – and already he had given him candy on several occasions, as well as a metal pencil with red lead in it – he could not bring himself to accept his being a part of the household. And then there were the singular visits of strange, rich townspeople, persons whom his aunt never had known, but who now appeared to find it quite natural to come to the house, stay for five or ten minutes talking to Señor Ong, and then go away again without so much as asking after his aunt, who always made a point of being in the back of the house or in the garden when they came. He could not understand that at all. It was still her house. Or perhaps not! Maybe she had given it to Señor Ong. Women often were crazy. He did not dare ask her. Once he was able to bring himself to inquire about the people, who kept coming in increasing numbers. She had answered: 'They are friends of Señor Ong', and had looked at him with an expression which seemed to say: 'Is that enough for you, busybody?' He was more than ever convinced that there was something more to know about the visitors. Then he met Luz, and being no longer alone, he ceased for a time to think about them.

When, one windy day, he had first seen her standing on the bridge, her bright head shining against the black mountains behind, he had stopped walking and stood perfectly still in order to look more carefully; he thought there was a mistake in his seeing. Never would he have believed it possible for anyone to look that way. Her hair was a silky white helmet on the top of her head, her whole face was white, almost as if she had covered it with paint, her brows and lashes, and even her eyes, were light to the point of not existing. Only her pale pink lips seemed real. She clutched the railing of the bridge tightly, an expression of intense preoccupation – or perhaps faint pain – on her face as she peered out from beneath her inadequate white brows. And her head moved slowly up and down as if it were trying to find an angle of vision which would be bearable for those feeble eyes that suffered behind their white lashes.

A few weeks back he merely would have stood looking at this apparition; now he watched intently until the girl, who was about his own age, seemed on the point of pitching forward into the road, and then he hurried toward her and firmly took her arm. An instant she drew back, squinting into his face.

'Who?' she said, confused.

'Me. What's the matter?'

She relaxed, let herself be led along. 'Nothing,' she answered after a moment. Nicho walked with her down the path to the river. When they got to the shade, the heavy lines in her forehead disappeared. 'The sun hurts your eyes?' he asked her, and she said that it did. Under a giant breadfruit tree there were clean grey rocks; they sat down and he began a series of questions. She answered placidly; her name was Luz; she had come with her sister only two days ago from San Lucas; she would stay on with her grandfather here because her parents were having quarrels at home. All her replies were given while she gazed out across the landscape, yet Nicho was sure she could not see the feathery trees across the river or the mountains beyond. He asked her: 'Why don't you look at me when you talk to me?'

She put her hand in front of her face. 'My eyes are ugly.'

'It's not true!' he declared with indignation. Then, 'They're beautiful,' he added, after looking at them carefully for a moment.

She saw that he was not making fun of her, and straight away decided that she liked him more than any boy she had ever known.

That night he told his aunt about Luz, and as he described the colours in her face and hair he saw her look pleased. '*Una hija del sol!*' she exclaimed. 'They bring good luck. You must invite her here tomorrow. I shall prepare her a good *refresco de tamarindo*.' Nicho said he would, but he had no intention of subjecting his friend to his aunt's interested scrutiny. And while he was not at all astonished to hear that albinos had special powers, he thought it selfish of his aunt to want to profit immediately by those which Luz might possess.

The next day when he went to the bridge and found Luz standing there, he was careful to lead her through a hidden lane down to the water, so that she might remain unseen as they passed near the house. The bed of the river lay largely in the shadows cast by the great trees that grew along its sides. Slowly the two children wandered downstream, jumping from rock to rock. Now and then they startled a vulture, which rose at their approach like a huge cinder, swaying clumsily in the air while they walked by, to realight in the same spot a moment later. There was a particular place that he wanted to show her, where the river widened and had sandy shores, but it lay a good way downstream, so that it took them a long time to get there. When they arrived, the sun's light was golden and the insects had begun to call. On the hill, invisible behind the thick wall of trees, the soldiers were having machine-gun practice: the blunt little berries of sound came in clusters at irregular intervals. Nicho rolled his trouser-legs up high above his knees and waded well out into the shallow stream. 'Wait!' he called to her. Bending, he scooped up a handful of sand from the river bed. His attitude as he brought it back for her to see was so triumphant that she caught her breath, craned her neck to see it before he had arrived. arrived.

'What is it?' she asked.

'Look! Silver!' he said, dropping the wet sand reverently into her outstretched palm. The tiny grains of mica glistened in the late sunlight.

'*Qué precioso!*' she cried in delight. They sat on some roots by the water. When the sand was drier, she poured it carefully into the pocket of her dress.

'What are you going to do with it?' he asked her.

'Give it to my grandfather.'

'No, no!' he exclaimed. 'You don't give away silver. You hide it. Don't you have a place where you hide things?'

Luz was silent; she never had thought of hiding anything. 'No,' she said presently, and she looked at him with admiration.

He took her hand. 'I'll give you a special place in my garden where you can hide everything you want. But you must never tell anyone.'

'Of course not.' She was annoyed that he should think her so stupid. For a while she had been content just to sit there with Nicho beside her; now she was impatient to get back and deposit the treasure. He tried to persuade her to stay a little longer, saying that there would be time enough if they returned later, but she had stood up and would not sit down again. They climbed upstream across the boulders, coming suddenly upon a pool where two young women stood thigh-deep washing clothes, naked save for the skirts wrapped round their waists, long full skirts that floated gently in the current. The women laughed and called out a greeting. Luz was scandalized.

'They should be ashamed!' she cried. 'In San Lucas if a woman did that, everyone would throw stones at her until she was buried under them!'

'Why?' said Nicho, thinking that San Lucas must be a very wicked town.

'Because they would,' she answered, still savouring the shock and shame she had felt at the sight of the golden breasts in the sunlight.

When they got back to town they turned into the path that led to Nicho's house, and while they were still in the jungle end of the garden, Nicho stopped and indicated a dead tree whose trunk had partially decayed. With the gesture of a conspirator he pulled aside the fringed curtain of vines that hung down across most of it, revealing several dark holes. Reaching into one of them, he pulled out a bright tin can, flicked off the belligerent ants that raced wildly around it, and held it forth to her.

'Put it in here,' he whispered.

It took a while to transfer all the sand from her pocket to the can; when it was done he replaced it inside the dark trunk and let the vines fall straight again to cover the place. Then he conducted Luz quickly up through the garden, around the house, into the street. His aunt, having caught sight of them, called: 'Dionisio!' But he pretended not to have heard her and pushed Luz ahead of him nervously. He was suddenly in terror lest Luz see Señor Ong; that was something which must be avoided at any cost.

'Dionisio!' She was still calling; she had come out and was standing in front of the door, looking down the street after them, but he did not turn around. They reached the bridge. It was out of sight of the house.

'*Adiós*,' he said.

'*Hasta mañana*,' she answered, peering up at him with her strange air of making a great effort. He watched her walk up the street, moving her head from side to side as if there were a thousand things to see, when in reality there were only a few pigs and some chickens roaming about.

At the evening meal his aunt eyed him reproachfully. He averted her gaze; she did not mention his promise to bring Luz to the house for *refrescos*. That night he lay on his mat watching the phosphorescent beetles. His room gave on to the patio; it had only three walls. The fourth side was wide open. Branches of the lemon tree reached in and rubbed against the wall above his head; up there, too, was a huge unfolding banana leaf which was pushing its way further into the room each day. Now the patio was dizzy with the beetles' sharp lights. Crawling on the plants or flying frantically between them, they flashed their signals on and off with maddening insistence. In the neighbouring room his aunt and Señor Ong occupied the bed of the house, enjoying the privacy of quarters that were closed in on all four sides. He listened: the wind was rising. Nightly it appeared and played on the leaves of the trees, dying away again before dawn. Tomorrow he would take Luz down to the river to get more silver. He hoped Señor Ong had not been spying when he had uncovered the holes in the tree trunk. The mere thought of such a possibility set him to worrying, and he twisted on his mat from one side to the other.

Presently he decided to go and see if the silver was still there. Once he had assured himself either that it was safe or that it had been stolen, he would feel better about it. He sat up, slipped into his trousers, and stepped out into the patio. The night was full of life and motion; leaves and branches touched, making tiny sighs. Singing insects droned in the trees overhead; everywhere the bright beetles flashed. As he stood there feeling the small wind wander over him he became aware of other sounds in the direction of the *sala*. The light was on there, and for a moment he thought that perhaps Señor Ong had a late visitor, since that was the room where he received his callers. But he heard no voices. Avoiding the lemon tree's sharp twigs, he made his way soundlessly to the closed doors and peered between them.

There was a square niche in the *sala* wall across which, when he had first arrived, Señor Ong had tacked a large calendar. This bore a coloured picture of a smiling Chinese girl. She wore a blue bathing suit and white fur-topped boots, and she sat by a pool of shiny pink tiles. Over her head in a luminous sky a gigantic four-motored plane bore down upon her, and further above, in a still brighter area of the heavens, was the benevolent face of Generalissimo Chiang. Beneath the picture were the words: ABARROTES FINOS. Sun Man Ngai, Huixtla, Chis. The calendar was the one object Señor Ong had brought with him that Nicho could wholeheartedly admire; he knew every detail of the picture by heart. Its presence had transformed the *sala* from a dull room with two old rocking-chairs and a table to a place where anything might happen if one waited long enough. And now as he peeked through the crack, he saw with a shock that Señor Ong had removed the calendar from its place on the wall, and laid it on the table. He had a hammer and a chisel and he was pounding and scratching the bottom of the niche. Occasionally he would scoop out the resulting plaster and dust with his fat little hands, and dump it in a neat pile on the table. Nicho waited for a long time without daring to move. Even when the wind blew a little harder and chilled his naked back he did not stir, for fear of seeing Señor Ong turn around and look with his narrow eyes toward the door, the hammer in one hand, the chisel in the other. Besides, it was important to know what he was doing. But Señor Ong seemed to be in no hurry. Almost an hour went by, and still tirelessly he kept up his methodical work, pausing regularly to take out the debris and pile it on the table. At last Nicho began to feel like sneezing; in a frenzy he turned and ran through the patio to his room, scratching his chest against the branches on the way. The emotion engendered by his flight had taken away his desire to sneeze, but he lay down anyway for fear it might return if he went back to the door. In the midst of wondering about Señor Ong he fell asleep.

The next morning when he went into the *sala* the pretty Chinese girl covered the niche as usual. He stood still listening: his aunt and Señor Ong were talking in the next room. Quickly he pulled out the thumbtack in the lower left-hand corner of the calendar and reached in. He could feel nothing there. Disappointed, he fastened it back and went out into the garden. In the tree his treasure was undisturbed, but now that he suspected Señor Ong of having a treasure too, the little can of sand seemed scarcely worth his interest.

He went to the bridge and waited for Luz. When she came they walked to the river below the garden and sat beside the water. Nicho's mind was full of the image of Señor Ong bending over the niche with his tools, and his fancy was occupied with speculation as to what exactly he had been doing. He was uncertain whether or not to share his secret with Luz. He hoped she would not talk about her silver this morning; to forestall inquiries about it he mentioned curtly that he had looked at it only a half hour ago and that it was intact. Luz sat regarding him perplexedly; he seemed scarcely the same person as yesterday. Finally she said, as he continued to fix his gaze on the black pebbles at his feet: 'What's the matter with you today?'

'Nothing.' He grasped her arm to belie his word; the gesture betrayed him into beginning the confidence. 'Listen. In my house there's a lot of gold hidden.' He told her everything: Señor Ong's arrival, his own dislike of him, the visits of the town's rich shopkeepers to the house, and finally the suspicious behaviour of Señor Ong in the *sala* the night before. She listened, blinking rapidly all the while. And when he had finished she agreed with him that it was probably gold hidden there in the niche; only she was inclined to think that it belonged to his aunt, and that Señor Ong had stolen it from her. This idea has not occurred to Nicho, and he did not really believe it. Nevertheless, it pleased him. 'I'll get it and give it back to her,' he declared.

'Of course,' said Luz solemnly, as if there were no alternative.

They sat a while without speaking. Up in the garden all the cockatoos were screaming at once. The prospect of stealing back the gold in order to return it to his aunt excited him. But there were dangers. He began to describe the hideousness of Señor Ong's person and character, extemporaneously adding details. Luz shivered and looked apprehensively toward the shadowy path. '*Hay que tener mucho cuidado,*' she murmured. Then suddenly she wanted to go home.

Now there was only one thing to wait for: Señor Ong's absence from the house. In Tlaltepec there lived a Chinese man whom he usually visited each week, going on the early bus in the morning and returning in time for the midday meal. Three days went by. People came to the house and went away again, but Señor Ong sat quietly in the *sala* without once going into the street. Each day Nicho and Luz met on the bridge and sat by the river discussing the treasure with an excitement that steadily grew. '*Ay, qué maravilla!*' she would exclaim, holding her hands far apart. 'This much gold!' Nicho would nod in agreement; all the same he had a feeling that when he saw the treasure he would be disappointed.

Finally the morning came when Señor Ong kissed Nicho's aunt on the cheek and went out of the house carrying a newspaper under his arm. 'Where is he going?' Nicho asked innocently.

'Tlaltepec.' His aunt was scrubbing the floor of the *sala*.

He went into the patio and watched a humming-bird buzz from one to another of the *huele-de-noche*'s white flowers. When his aunt had finished in the *sala* she shut the door and started on the floor of the bedroom. In agitation he tiptoed into the room and over to the calendar, whose two lower corners he unfastened from the wall. Again the niche was empty. Its floor consisted of four large flower-decorated tiles. Without touching them he could tell which was the loose one. He lifted it up and felt underneath. It was a paper packet, not very large, and, which was worse, soft to the touch. He pulled out a fat manila envelope, replaced the tile and the calendar, and walked softly out through the patio, into the garden to his tree.

In the large envelope were a lot of little envelopes, and in some of the little envelopes there was a small quantity of odourless white powder. The other little envelopes were empty, held together by a rubber band. That was all there was. Nicho had expected a disappointment, but scarcely so complete a one as this. He was furious: Señor Ong had played a joke on him, had replaced the gold with this worthless dust, just out of devilry. But when he thought about it, he decided that Señor Ong could not have guessed that he knew about the niche, so that after all this powder must be the real treasure. Also he felt it unlikely that it belonged to his aunt, in which case Señor Ong would be even more angry to find it gone. He took out two of the small empty envelopes, and from each of the others he poured a tiny bit of powder, until these two also contained about the same amount. Then he replaced both empty and full envelopes in the larger folder, and seeing that his aunt was in the kitchen, went back to the *sala* with it. Señor Ong would never notice the two missing envelopes or the powder that Nicho had poured into them. Once back in the garden he hid the two tiny packets under the tin can full of sand, and wandered down to the bridge.

It was too early to expect Luz. A tiny grey curtain of rain came drifting up the valley. In another few minutes it would have arrived. The green mountainside at the end of the street glared in the half light. Don Anastasio came walking jauntily down the main street, and turned in at the side street where Nicho's house was. Obeying a blind impulse, he called to him: '*Muy buenos, Don Anastasio!*' The old man wheeled about; he seemed none too pleased to see Nicho. 'Good day,' he replied, and then he hurried on. Nicho ran from the bridge and stood at the entrance of the street watching him. Sure enough, he was about to go into Nicho's house.

'Don Anastasio!' he shouted, beginning to run toward him.

Don Anastasio stopped walking and stood still, his face screwed up in annoyance. Nicho arrived out of breath. 'You wanted to see Señor Ong? He's gone out.'

Don Anastasio did not look happy now, either. 'Where?' he said heavily.

'I think to Mapastenango, perhaps,' said Nicho, trying to sound vague, and wondering if that could be counted as a lie.

'*Qué malo!*' grunted Don Anastasio. 'He won't be back today, then.'

'I don't know.'

There was a silence.

'Can I do anything for you?' faltered Nicho.

'No, no,' said Don Anastasio hastily; then he stared down at him. During the week when Nicho had been working at his store, he had had occasion to notice that the boy was unusually quick. 'That is,' he added slowly, 'I don't suppose – did Señor Ong . . .?'

'Just a minute,' said Nicho, feeling that he was about to discover the secret and at the same time become master of the situation. 'Wait here,' he added firmly. At the moment Don Anastasio showed no inclination to do anything else. He stood watching Nicho disappear around the corner of the house.

In a minute the boy returned panting, and smiled at Don Anastasio.

'Shall we go to the bridge?' he said.

Again Don Anastasio acquiesced, looking furtively up and down the long street as they came out into it. They stood on the bridge leaning over the water below, and Nicho brought one of the little envelopes out of his pocket, glancing up at Don Anastasio's face at the same time. Yes! He had been right! He saw the features fixed in an expression of relief, pleasure and greedy anticipation. But only for an instant. By the time he was handing over the packet to Don Anastasio, the old man's face looked the same as always.

'*Muy bien, muy bien,*' he grumbled. The first small drops of rain alighted softly on their heads, but neither noticed them. 'Do I pay you or Señor Ong?' said Don Anastasio, pocketing the envelope.

Nicho's heart beat harder for a few seconds: Señor Ong must not know of this. But he could not ask Don Anastasio not to tell him. He cleared his throat and said: 'Me.' But his voice sounded feeble.

'Aha!' said Don Anastasio, smiling a little; and he ruffled Nicho's hair in paternal fashion. Finding it wet, he looked up vacantly at the sky. 'It's raining,' he commented, a note of surprise in his voice.

'*Sí, señor,*' assented Nicho weakly.

'How much?' said Don Anastasio, looking at him very hard. In the valley the thunder groaned faintly.

Nicho felt he must answer immediately, but he had no idea what to say. 'Is a peso all right?'

Don Anastasio stared at him even harder; he felt that the old man's eyes would cut through him in another instant. Then Don Anastasio's countenance changed suddenly, and he said: 'A peso. Good.' And he handed him a silver coin. 'Next week you come to my store with another envelope. I'll give you an extra twenty centavos for making the trip. And – sssst!' He put his fingers to his lips, rolling his eyes upward. 'Ssst!' He patted Nicho on the shoulder, looking very pleased, and went up the street.

Señor Ong came back earlier than usual, wet through, and in rather a bad humour. Nicho never had paid any attention to the conversations that passed between his aunt and Señor Ong. Now from the kitchen he listened, and heard him say:

'I have no confidence in Ha. They tell me he was in town here two days ago. Of course he swears he was in Tlaltepec all the time.'

'Three thousand pesos thrown into the street!' declared his aunt savagely. 'I told you so then. I told you he would go on selling here as well as in Tlaltepec. *Yo te lo dije, hombre!*'

'I am not sure yet,' said Señor Ong, and Nicho could imagine his soft smile as he said the words. Now that he had stolen from him he disliked him more than ever; in a sense he almost wished Señor Ong might discover the theft and accuse him, thereby creating the opportunity for him to say: 'Yes, I stole from you, and I hate you.' But he knew that he himself would do nothing to hasten such a moment. He went out through the rain to his tree. The earth's dark breath rose all around him, hung in the wet air. He took out the can of sand and dropped the peso into it.

It rained all day and through the night; Nicho did not see Luz until the following day. Then he adopted a mysterious, baffled air and conducted her to the tree.

'Look!' he cried, showing her the tin can. 'The silver has made a peso!'

Luz was convinced and delighted, but she did not seem really surprised. '*Qué bueno!*' she murmered.

'Do you want to take it?' He held up the coin. But he was careful to keep his hand over the envelope in the tree's hollow.

'No, no! Leave it! Maybe it will make more. Put it back! Put it back!'

He was a little crestfallen to find that she took his miracle so nearly for granted. They stamped their feet to knock off the ants that were beginning to climb up their legs.

'And the gold?' she whispered. 'Did you get it back for your aunt? Was it heavy? What did Señor Ong say?'

'There was nothing there at all,' said Nicho, feeling uncomfortable without knowing why.

'Oh.' She was disappointed.

They took a long walk down the river, and came upon an enormous iguana sunning himself on a rock above a pool. Nicho threw a stone, and the monster lumbered away into the leaves. Luz clutched his arm tightly as it disappeared from sight; there was the heavy sound of its body dragging through the underbrush. All at once Nicho shook himself free, pulled off his shirt and trousers, and gave a running leap into the pool. He splashed about, beating wildly at the water with his arms and legs, yelling loudly all the while. With an uncertain gait Luz approached the edge, where she sat down and watched him. Presently she said: 'Find some more silver.' She did not seem at all shocked by his nudity. He sank to the bottom and scrabbled about, touching only rock. Up again, he shouted: 'There isn't any!' Her white head followed his movements as he cavorted around the pool. When he came out, he sat on the opposite side, letting the sun dry him. Behind the hill the machine-gun practice was again in progress.

'In San Lucas do you think they'd throw stones at me?' he shouted.

'Why?' she called. 'No, no! *Claro que nó!* For boys it's all right.'

The next few days were sunny, and they came each afternoon to the pool.

One morning, the other little envelope in his pocket, Nicho went into the centre of town to Don Anastasio's shop. The old man seemed very glad to see him. He opened the envelope behind the counter and looked carefully at its contents. Then he handed Nicho a peso and a half.

'I have no change,' said Nicho.

'The *tostón* is for you,' said Don Anastasio gruffly. 'There's a cinema tonight. Come back next week. Don't forget.'

Nicho ran down the street, wondering when he would have the chance to fill another envelope for Don Anastasio. It was about time for Señor Ong to make a trip to Tlaltepec.

A moment before he got to the bridge a tall woman stepped out of a shop and confronted him. She had very large eyes and a rather frightening face.

'*Hola, chico!*'

'*Sí, señora.*' He stood still and stared at her.

'Have you got something for me?'

'Something for you?' he repeated blankly.

'A little envelope?' She held out two pesos.

Nicho looked at them and said: '*No, señora.*'

Her face became more frightening. 'Yes. Yes. You have,' she insisted, moving toward him. He glanced up and down the street: there was no one. The shop seemed to be empty. It was the hot hour of the day. ·

He was suddenly terrified by her face. 'Tomorrow,' he cried, ducking to one side in order to dart past her.

But she caught hold of his neck. 'Today,' she said roughly; her long fingernails were pushing into his skin.

'*Sí, señora.*' He did not dare look up at her.

'On the bridge,' she grated. 'This afternoon.'

'*Sí, señora.*'

She let go and he walked on, sobbing a little with anger and shame for having been afraid.

In the *sala* Señor Ong and his aunt were talking excitedly. He did not go in, but climbed into a hammock in the patio and listened. Don Anastasio's name was mentioned. Nicho's heart skipped ahead: something had happened!

'Now I am almost sure,' Señor Ong said slowly. 'It is two weeks since he has been here, and Saenz tells me he is perfectly happy. That means only one thing: Ha must be supplying him directly.'

'Of course,' said his aunt bitterly. 'You needn't have waited two weeks to know that. Three thousand pesos dropped into the river. What a waste! *Qué idiota, tú!*'

Señor Ong paid no attention to her. 'There's also the Fernandez woman,' he mused. 'She should have been around a few days ago. I know she has no money, but so far she has always managed to scrape together something.'

'That old hag!' said his aunt contemptuously. 'With her face now, she'll be lucky if she can raise twenty, not to speak of fifty.'

'She can raise it,' said Señor Ong with confidence in his voice. 'The question is, has Ha already found her and is he giving it to her for less?'

'Don't ask *me* all these questions!' cried his aunt with impatience. 'Go to Tlaltepec and ask the old man himself!'

'When I go there,' said Señor Ong in a quiet, deadly voice, 'it will not be to ask him anything.'

At that moment a knock came on the front door; his aunt immediately left the room, shutting the door behind her, and went through the patio into the kitchen. For a few minutes Nicho could hear only the confused sound of low voices talking in the *sala*. Presently someone closed the front door. The visitor was gone.

Before the midday meal Nicho went out into the garden and tossed the two silver coins Don Anastasio had given him into the can of sand. It gave him pleasure to think of showing them to Luz; her credulity made him feel clever and superior. He determined never to tell her about the powder. All through lunch he thought about the tall woman he was to meet on the bridge. When the meal was over, Señor Ong did something unusual: he took up his hat and said: 'I am going to see Saenz and have a talk with him.' And he went out. Nicho watched him disappear into the main street; then he went into the house and saw his aunt shut herself into the bedroom for her siesta. Without hesitating he walked straight to the niche in the *sala* and took out the big yellow envelope. He knew he was doing a dangerous thing, but he was determined to do it anyway. Quickly he slipped two fat little envelopes into his pocket. He left one in his tree, and with the other he went out and stood on the bridge to wait for the woman. She was not long in spotting him from the shop. As she came toward him, her haggard face seemed to darken the afternoon. He held the little white envelope out to her even as she approached, as if to keep her at a certain distance from him. Frowning mightily, she reached for it, snatched it from his fingers like a furious bird, and violently pushed it inside her bodice. With the other hand she put two pesos into his still outstretched palm; and then she strode away without saying a word. He decided to remain on the bridge, hoping that Luz would appear presently.

When she came, he suddenly did not want to take her to the tree, or even to the river. Instead, grasping her hand, he said: 'I have an idea.' This was not true; as yet he had no idea, but he felt the need of doing something new, important.

'What idea?'

'Let's take a trip!'

'A trip! Where to?'

They started up the street hand in hand.

'We can take a bus,' he said.

'But where?'

'*No importa adonde.*'

Luz was not convinced the idea was sound; her mind was encumbered with visions of her older sister's stern face when she returned. Nevertheless he could see that she would go. As they came to where the houses and shops began, he let go of her hand for fear of meeting one of his friends. He had never walked on the street with her. The sun's light was intense, but a gigantic white cloud was rising slowly up from behind the mountains in front of them. He turned to look at her pale shining head. Her eyes were painful, squinting slits in her face. Surely no one else in the world had such beautiful hair. Glancing at the cloud he whispered to her: 'The sun will go in soon.'

At the central plaza there was a bus half full of people. From time to time the driver, who stood leaning against its red tin body, shouted: 'Tlaltepec! Tlaltepec!' No sooner had they got aboard and taken seats near the back alongside the windows than Luz, in an access of apprehensiveness, asked to get out. But he held her arm and said, hurriedly inventing: '*Oye*, I wanted to go to Tlaltepec because we have something very important to do there. We have to save somebody's life.' She listened attentively to his story: the monstrous Señor Ong was going to kill old Señor Ha for not having kept his promise to stay in Tlaltepec. As he recounted the tale, and recalled the wording of Señor Ong's threat, he began to believe the story himself. 'When I go there it will not be to ask him anything.' The old man would be given no opportunity to explain, no chance to defend himself. As the bus moved out of the plaza, he was as convinced as Luz that they were off to Tlaltepec on an heroic mission.

Tlaltepec was below, in a closed valley with mountains on all sides. The great white cloud, its brilliant edges billowing outward, climbed higher into the sky; as into a cave, the bus entered the precinct of its shadow. Here suddenly everything was green. Scraps of bird-song came in through the open windows, sharp above the rattling of the ancient vehicle.

'*Ay, el pobrecito!*' sighed Luz from time to time.

They came into Tlaltepec, stopped in the plaza. The passengers got out and quickly dispersed in different directions. The village was very quiet. Bright green grass grew in the middle of the streets. A few silent Indians sat around the plaza against the walls. Nicho and Luz walked up the main street, awed by the hush which enveloped the village. The cloud had covered the sky; now it was slowly pulled down like a curtain over the other side of the valley. A sad little churchbell began to ring behind them in the plaza. They turned into a small shop marked *Farmacia Moderna*. The man sitting inside knew Señor Ha: he was the only Chinese in the village. 'He lives opposite the convent, in the last house.' In Tlaltepec everything was near by. The bell was still tolling from the plaza. In front of the ruined convent was an open square of sward; basketball posts had been put up at each end, but now they were broken. Before the last house stood a large tree laden with thousands of lavender flowers. In the still air they fell without cease, like silent tears, on to the damp earth beneath.

Nicho knocked on the door. A servant girl came and looked at the two children indifferently, went away. In a moment Señor Ha appeared. He was not quite so old as they had expected; his angular face was expressionless, but he looked closely at both of them. Nicho had hoped he would ask them into the house: he wanted to see if Señor Ha had a calendar like the one at home in the *sala*, but no such hospitality was forthcoming. Luz sat down on the stone step below them and picked up some of the blossoms that had fallen from the tree while Nicho told Señor Ha who he was and why he had come. Señor Ha stood quite still. Even when Nicho said: 'And he is going to kill you', his hard little eyes remained in exactly the same position. Nothing in his face moved; he looked at Nicho as though he had not heard a word. For a moment Nicho thought that perhaps he understood nothing but Chinese, but then Señor Ha said, very clearly: 'What lies!' And he shut the door.

They walked back to the plaza without saying anything, and sat down on an iron bench to wait for the bus. A warm, mistlike rain moved downward through the air, falling so softly that it was inaudible even in the stillness of the deserted plaza. At one point while they waited Nicho got up and went to the main street in search of some candy. As he came out of the shop, a little man carrying a briefcase walked quickly past and crossed the street. It was Señor Ha.

While they sat eating the candy a battered sedan came out of the main street and bumped across the plaza; on the edge of its back seat, leaning forward talking to the driver, was Señor Ha. They stared. The car turned into the road that led up the mountainside toward the town, and disappeared in the twilight.

'He's going to tell Señor Ong!' cried Nicho suddenly. He let his mouth stay open and fixed the ground.

Luz squeezed his arm. 'You don't care,' she declared. 'They're only Chinamen. You're not afraid of them.'

He looked blankly at her. Then with scorn he answered: 'No!'

They talked very little on the ride up in the rain. It was night by the time they arrived in the town. Wet and hungry, they went down the street toward the bridge, still without speaking. As they crossed the river Nicho turned to her and said: 'Come and have dinner at my house.'

'My sister . . .'

But he pulled her roughly along with him. Even as he opened the front door and saw his aunt and Señor Ong sitting inside, he knew that Señor Ha had not been there.

'Why are you so late?' said his aunt. 'You're wet.' Then she saw Luz. 'Shut the door, *niña*,' she said, looking pleased.

While they ate in the covered part of the patio, Señor Ong continued with what he apparently had been saying earlier in the evening. . . . 'She looked directly at me without saying a word.'

'Who?' said his aunt, smiling at Luz.

'The Fernandez woman. This afternoon.' Señor Ong's voice was edged with impatience. 'For me that is proof enough. She's getting it somewhere else.'

His aunt snorted. 'Still you're looking for proof! *Niña*, take more meat.' She piled extra food on Luz's plate.

'Yes, there's no doubt now,' Señor Ong continued.

'What beautiful hair! *Ay, Dios!*' She smoothed the top of the girl's head. Nicho was ashamed: he knew that he had invited her to dinner because he had been afraid to come home alone, and he knew that his aunt was touching her hair only in order to bring herself good luck. He sighed miserably and glanced at Luz; she seemed perfectly content as she ate.

Suddenly there were several loud knocks on the front door. Sēnor Ong rose and went into the *sala*. There was a silence. A man's voice said: '*Usted se llama Narciso Ong?*' All at once there followed a great deal of noise; feet scuffled and furniture scraped on the tile floor. Nicho's aunt jumped up and ran into the kitchen where she began to pray very loudly. In the *sala* there was grunting and wheezing, and then as the racket grew less intense, a man said: '*Bueno*. I have it. A hundred grams, at least, right in his pocket. That's all we needed, my friend. *Vamonos.*'

Nicho slid down from his chair and stood in the doorway. Two men in wet brown ponchos were pushing Señor Ong out the front door. But he did not seem to want to go. He twisted his head and saw Nicho, opened his mouth to speak to him. One of the men hit him in the side of the face with his fist. 'Not in front of the boy,' said Señor Ong, wriggling his jaw back and forth to see if it was all right. 'Not in front of the boy,' he said again thickly. The other man slammed the door shut. The *sala* was empty. There was no sound but his aunt's wailing voice in the kitchen, crying aloud to God. He turned to look at Luz, who was sitting perfectly still.

'Do you want to go home?' he said to her.

'Yes.' She got up. His aunt came out of the kitchen wringing her hands. Going over to Luz she laid her hand briefly on the white hair, still muttering a prayer.

'*Adiós, niña*. Come back tomorrow,' she said.

There was still a light rain falling. A few insects sang from the wet leaves as the two silent children passed along the way to the house where Luz lived. When they rapped on the door it was opened immediately. A tall thin girl stood there. Without speaking she seized Luz with one arm and pulled her violently inside, closing the door with the other.

When Nicho got home and went into the *sala*, his first thought was that Señor Ong had returned, but the next instant he felt that he was in the middle of a bad dream. Señor Ha was sitting there talking with his aunt. She looked up tearfully. 'Go to bed,' she commanded.

Señor Ha reached out from his chair as Nicho passed and

caught his arm – caught it very tightly. '*Ay!*' said Nicho in spite of himself. 'One moment,' said Señor Ha, still looking at Nicho's aunt, and never for a second relaxing his grip. 'Perhaps this one knows.' And without turning his face toward Nicho he said: 'The police have taken Señor Ong to prison. He will not come back here. He hid something in this house. Where is it?'

It seemed as though the hard fingers would cut through his skin. His aunt looked up at him hopefully. He felt suddenly very important.

'There,' he said, pointing to the calendar.

Señor Ha rose and yanked the pretty girl down from the wall. In an instant he had the yellow envelope in his hand. As he examined its contents, he said: 'Is there any more?'

'No,' said Nicho, thinking of the envelope lying in the safety of his tree out there in the rainy night. Señor Ha began to twist his arm, but the thought of his secret made him feel strong; his pain and his hatred flowed into that feeling of strength. He stood stiffly and let Señor Ha hurt him. A moment later Señor Ha let go of him and gave him a violent push that sent him half-way across the room. 'Go to bed,' he said.

When Nicho had gone out and closed the door, Señor Ha turned to the aunt. 'Tomorrow I shall come back with my clothes,' he said. 'It is not good to have a boy around the house doing nothing; he gets into trouble. From now on he will deliver it; there will be no one coming to the house.'

'But if the police catch him . . .' she objected.

'There will be no trouble with them. It is all arranged. Fortunately I had nearly three thousand pesos on hand.' He picked up his briefcase and went to the door. She looked after him with frank admiration and sighed deeply. 'You won't stay tonight?' She said the words timidly, and they sounded strangely coquettish.

'No. The car is outside waiting for me. Tomorrow.' He opened the door. Rising, she went and took his hand, pressing it warmly between her two hands. 'Tomorrow,' he repeated.

When the car had driven away and she could no longer hear it, she closed the door, turned off the light, and went out into the patio, where she got into a hammock and lay swinging gently back and forth.

An intelligent man, she said to herself. What good luck! She stopped swinging a moment. Good luck! Of course! Dionisio must bring her to the house again one day very soon.

The town went on being prosperous, the Indians kept coming down from the heights with money, the thick jungle along the way to Mapastenango was hacked away, the trail widened and improved. Nicho bought a packet of little envelopes. Far down the river he found another hollow tree. Here he kept his slowly increasing store of treasure; during the very first month he picked up enough money on the side to buy Luz a lipstick and a pair of dark glasses with red and green jewels all around the rims.

Tapiama

Just behind the hotel was the river. If it had come from very far inland it would have been wide and silent, but because it was really only a creek swollen by the rains, and its bed was full of boulders, it made a roaring noise which the photographer briefly mistook for more rain. The heat and the trip had tired him out; he had eaten the cold fried fish and the leathery omelette that oozed grease, the brown bean paste with rice and burned bananas, and had been overtaken suddenly by a sleepiness powerful as the effect of a drug. Staggering to his bed, he had ripped off his shirt and trousers, lifted the stiff mosquito-net that reeked of dust, and dropped like a stone on to the mattress, only distantly noticing its hardness before he lost himself in sleep.

But in the night when he awoke he realized he had been in the false sleep of indigestion; staring into the blackness over his head he told himself that it was going to be hard to find the way back into oblivion. It was then that he had become aware of the night's changeless backdrop of sound, and had taken it for rain. Now and then, far above his head (how could the ceiling be that high?) a firefly's nervous little light flashed its indecipherable code for an instant or two. He was lying on his back; something small was crawling down his chest. He put his hand there: it was a slowly moving drop of sweat. The rough sheet under him was wet. He wanted to move, but if he did there would be no end to the shifting, and each new position would be more uncomfortable than the last. In the anonymous darkness of a nearby room someone coughed from time to time; he could not tell whether it was a man or a woman. The meal he had eaten lay like ten meals in

131

his stomach. Slowly the memory of it was being suffused with a nebulous horror – particularly the heavy cold omelette shining with grease.

Lying there smelling the dust from the netting was like being tied up inside a burlap bag. To get out into the street and walk – that was what he wanted, but there were difficulties. The electricity went off at midnight; the old man who ran the hotel had told him that. Instead of putting the matches under his pillow he had left them in his trouser-pocket, and the idea of stepping out on to the floor barefoot without a light did not appeal to him. Besides, he reminded himself, listening again to the wide, strangely distant clamour out there, it was raining. But to move along the dead streets even under the invisible rain would be a pleasure. . . . If he lay quite still, sleep might return. Finally, in desperation he yanked the net aside and sprang out of bed, across the room in the direction of the chair over which he had thrown his clothes.

He managed to get into his shirt and trousers in the space of three matches; his shoes he pounded on the concrete floor in the dark, to tumble out a possible centipede or scorpion. Then he struck a fourth match and opened the door into the patio. Here it was no longer pitch-black. The huge potted plants were visible in the night's lead-coloured light, but the sky, stifled by a cloud that no starlight could pierce, seemed not to be there at all. It was not raining. The river must be very close, he thought.

He walked along the covered *corredor*, grazing the tentacles of orchids that hung in baskets and jars from the eaves, bumping into the pieces of wicker furniture, and found the entrance door, closed and doubly bolted. Carefully he slid back the metal bars and opened the door, pulling it shut after him. The gloom of the street was as profound as that of the patio, and the air as still as it had been under the mosquito-net. But it had an indefinite vegetable scent – a sweet odour of both fulfilment and exhaustion.

He turned to the left: the long empty main street, lined with one-storey buildings, led straight down to the *paseo* along the sea. As he walked, the unmoving hot-house air became veined with the fresher smell of seaweed on the beach. At each intersecting street he had to go down six steps to the road level, cross, and climb up again to the sidewalk. In the rainy season, the *propietario* of the hotel had told him, there was a row-boat at each corner to ferry the pedestrians across. Like the intermingling of the land and sea odours that he breathed, two opposing but entwined sensations took possession of him: a relief amounting almost to delight, and a faint feeling of nausea which he decided to combat because he felt that not to have been able to leave all suggestion of illness behind showed a lack of strength. He tried to put more springiness into his walk, but discovered almost immediately that it was too hot to make any more than a minimum effort. He was sweating even more now than he had been in his bed. He lighted an Ovalado. The taste of the sweet black tobacco was a part of the night.

The *paseo* bordering the sea-front was about half a mile long. He had imagined there would be some slight stirring of the air here, but he could detect no difference. Still, now and then there was the soft intimate sound of a small wave breaking gently on the sand just below. He sat down on the balustrade and rested, in the hope of cooling off a little. The sea was invisible. He could have been sitting on the peak of a cloud-covered mountain – the gloom in front of him would have been that formless and all-embracing. Yet the sea's casual noises had no element of distance in them, as sea sounds have. It was as though they were taking place in a vast, closed courtyard. The concrete slabs on which he sat were damp, and a little cooler than his flesh. He smoked two cigarettes and strained his ears to hear some sound, made even indirectly, by human agency. But there was nothing more than the desultory slipping and sucking of the lazy water on the beach below. He glanced up and down the empty *paseo*. Far out along the shore to the west there was a light. It was orange, it flickered: a bonfire? He resumed walking, more slowly than before, ahead of him the distant blaze, the one point of light in the landscape.

A wide flight of steps led down on to the beach. Just beyond, he could see the flimsy structure of a pier that had been built out over the water. He stood still and listened. The fitful licking of small waves around the piles sounded as though it were happening in an echo-chamber.

He ran lightly down the steps and passed underneath the pier. It was definitely cooler walking along on the sand than it had been up on the *paseo*. He felt wide awake now, and decided to see how much nearer to the light down the shore fifteen minutes would put him. Night-coloured crabs hurried along the sand just ahead of his moving feet, completely soundless and almost invisible. A little beyond the end of the *paseo* the sand gave place to a hard coral surface which was easier to walk on. Out of prudence he kept as near to the water's edge as possible.

There was a difference between this walk and innumerable other midnight jaunts he had made, and he was inclined to wonder what made it so pleasant. Perhaps he was enjoying it simply because the fabric here was of pure freedom. He was not looking for anything; all the cameras were back in the hotel room.

Occasionally he lifted his eyes from the dim brainlike configurations of coral beneath his feet and looked inland, to see whether he could make out any signs of habitation. It seemed to him that there might be sand dunes a few hundred feet back, but in the absence of light it was impossible to be certain of even that much. The sweat trickled down his spine and over his coccyx, sliding in between his buttocks. Maybe the best idea would be to undress completely. But then there would be the bother of carrying his clothing, and he wanted his hands free, even at the risk of chafing.

The question of freedom was governed by the law of diminishing returns, he said to himself, walking faster. If you went beyond a certain point of intensity in your consciousness of desiring it, you furnished yourself with a guarantee of not achieving it. In any case, he thought, what is freedom in the last analysis, other than the state of being totally, instead of only partially, subject to the tyranny of chance?

There was no doubt that this walk was dispelling the miasma of indigestion that had lain within him. Three minutes to go, said the bright minute-hand of his watch; the orange light ahead seemed smaller than it had from the town. Why an arbitrary fifteen minutes? He smiled at the precise urban pattern in which his mind had automatically moved. If he lifted his arm he could touch the sky, and it would be moist, tepid and voluptuously soft.

And now in the distance ahead, on the landward side, he heard sounds which he quickly identified as the voices of hundreds of young frogs. The light, now that he studied it, was moving in a strange fashion: slightly up and down, and sideways as well, but without appearing to alter its position. All at once it became a huge flame belching upward, an instant later scattering cascades of red sparks, and he understood that he had arrived. The bonfire burned on the floor of a gently swaying craft not a hundred feet ahead of him. A naked man stood above it, tossing it palm branches. The photographer stopped walking and listened for the sound of human voices, but the happy chorus of frogs filled the air.

He stepped ahead several paces and decided to call out. '*Hola!*' The man wheeled about, jumped over the nearer side of the boat (the water was extremely shallow) and came running up to him.

Without greeting him, taking him perhaps for someone else, the man said: '*Tapiama? Vas a Tapiama?*' The photographer, never having heard of Tapiama, stuttered a bit and finally said: '*Sí,*' whereupon the other seized his arm and pulled him along to the edge of the water. 'The tide's all the way out. We'll start in a minute.'

He could see two other people in the craft, lying flat on the floor, one on each side of the fire, as far from its heat as possible. The photographer squatted down and removed his shoes and socks, then waded to the boat. When he stood in the centre of it (the fire was still crackling brightly) he turned and watched the naked man loosening the rope that held the craft in place.

'The whole thing is absurd.' He could only distrust the very naturalness with which all this was coming about – the indifference to his unexpected arrival on the part of the two passengers, and perhaps even more, the highly suspect readiness of the boatman to take off the moment he had appeared. He told himself: Things don't happen this way, but since beyond a doubt they were doing so, any questioning of the process could lead only in the direction of paranoia.

He dropped to the floor of the boat and pulled out his packet of Ovalados. The naked boatman, the coil of dripping rope around his black forearm like a bracelet, sprang aboard, and with his big toe nudged one of the supine passengers, who stirred, rose to his knees, and glanced about with annoyance. 'Where is it?' he demanded. Without replying, the boatman handed him the shorter of two poles that had lain along the gunwale. Together they began to propel the punt along the invisible surface of the water. The frogs' canticle and the fire's flare filled the night.

Having answered '*Sí*' to the Tapiama question, the photographer felt he could scarcely take the retrogressive step of asking 'What is Tapiama?' or 'Where is Tapiama?' And so, much as he would have liked to know, he decided to wait. This shallow body of water beneath them – estuary, lagoon? River more likely, since the boatman had said the tide was out. But not the stream whose troubled passage among the boulders he had heard from his bed.

They pushed on, now and then passing beneath clumps of high vegetation where the frogs' song was briefly covered by another sound, inexplicable and brutal, like the sudden tearing of a vast sheet of strong linen. From time to time something solid and heavy splashed near by, as if a man had fallen into the water. And occasionally the other passenger raised himself on one elbow and without too much effort managed to revive the dying fire with another dry palm-leaf.

Probably it was less than an hour before they came to a landing in the mud. The two passengers leaped out and hurried away into the darkness. The boatman, after carefully donning a pair of short underpants, tapped the photographer on the arm and asked him for sixty centavos. He gave him seventy-five and clambered out into the soft mud, his shoes in his hand.

'Wait a minute,' said the man. 'I'll go with you.' The photographer was pleased. When the boatman, looking blacker now in his white shorts, had secured the punt to an upright log driven into the mud, he led the way upward through a tangle of undergrowth, saying casually at one point: 'Are you going across tomorrow?'

'Across? No.'

'Aren't you here for the company?' The voice implied that to be here otherwise than for the company laid one open to unnameable suspicion.

The time had come to be truthful, he feared, although he did not relish the position he knew it would put him in. 'I never heard of the company,' he said. 'I just arrived in Rio Martillo tonight. What sort of company?'

'Sugar,' said the other. Then he stood still in the dark and spoke slowly: '*Entonces* – why have you come to Tapiama? They don't like *millonarios* here, you know.' Understanding that this was the contemptuous coastal term for Americans, the photographer quickly lied. 'I'm Danish,' he said, but feeling that his voice lacked conviction he immediately added: 'Do we go through any more mud, or can I put my shoes on?'

The man had started up again. 'Wash your feet at the *cantina*, if you like,' he told him over his shoulder. In another minute they were there; all in the dimness an open space, a dozen or so palm-leaf huts at one end of it, at the other a platform which must be a loading dock, the empty night and openness of water behind it; and half-way between the dock and the cluster of dwellings, the *cantina*, itself only a very large hut without a front wall.

A faint light came from within; there was no sound but the frogs on all sides, and the occasional tearing rasp in the branches high overhead. 'Why is the place open at this hour?' demanded the photographer. The boatman stopped in the middle of the clearing and adjusted his shorts briefly. 'Don Octavio runs it from six in the morning until six at night. His brother runs it from six at night until six in the morning. The company lets the men off from work at different hours. They come here with their *pago* and spend it. They like it better here than at home. Not so many mosquitoes.' It could have been the photographer's imagination that made the man's voice sound bitter as he spoke the last words. They continued across the clearing and stepped into the *cantina*.

There was no floor; the ground was covered with white sand. A counter of boards had been built diagonally across a far corner. Here an oil lamp smouldered and two men stood drinking. Wooden packing-cases were scattered here and there, some standing on end with empty beer bottles on them, and others on their sides, to be used as seats. '*Muy triste*,' commented the boatman, glancing around. Then he went behind the bar and disappeared through a small door in the wall there. Apart from the two at the bar, who had ceased their conversation and now stood staring at the photographer, there was no one else in the place. When in doubt, speak, he told himself, advancing towards them, although it occurred to him that he might just as well have made it: When in doubt, keep quiet, even as he opened his mouth to say: '*Buenas noches*', for their expressions did not alter in any manner that he could detect. For a full three seconds they continued to gaze at him before they replied, which they then did more or less simultaneously. These two had nothing in common, he noted: one was a soldier in uniform, an Indian boy of perhaps eighteen, the other a tired-looking mulatto civilian of indeterminate age. Or perhaps – the idea came to him as he put his elbow on the bar with a show of casualness – they did have at least a common antagonism, now that he had entered the *cantina*. Oh, well, I'm barefoot and my shoes are covered with mud, he thought.

'*Hay alguien?*' he said aloud to the palm-leaf wall behind the bar. The two neither resumed their conversation nor spoke further with him, and he did not turn his head again towards them. Presently the small door opened and a fat man pushed through. He stood with his hands outspread on the bar, his eyebrows raised in anticipation. 'I'll have a *cumbiamba*,' said the photographer, remembering the name of the coastal region's favourite drink, a herbal concoction famous for its treacherous effects.

It was foul-tasting but strong. The second one seemed less objectionable. He walked across to the open side of the *cantina* and sat down on a packing case, looking out at the formless night. The two at the bar were talking again now in low tones. It was not long before five men appeared from the platform end of the clearing; they straggled in and stood at the bar, laughing as they waited for their drinks. All of them were black, and wore only underpants, like the boatman. Now a mulatto girl with gold teeth came through the little door behind the bar and joined them. Almost immediately, however, she became aware of the photographer sitting by himself, and with her hands on her hips, half dancing, she made her way across the open space towards him. When she arrived, she squatted down beside him grinning and with one thin yellow hand reached out to unfasten his fly. His reaction was instantaneous and automatic: he drew back his leg and kicked her full in the breast, so that she toppled over backwards in silence on to the sand. The noise of the resulting laughter at the bar was not sufficient to cover her thin voice, made sharp by rage: '*Qué bruto, tú! Pendejo!*' Hands on hips again, she retreated to the bar and was given a beer by one of the workmen. Although the photographer had not meant to kick her, he felt no regret at the turn the incident had taken. The *cumbiambas* seemed to be having their effect; he was beginning to feel very well. He sat still a while, tapping rhythms on the side of his empty glass. Soon more Negro workmen came in and joined the others at the bar. One carried a guitar on which he set to work strumming a syncopated chordal accompaniment for a melody which failed to appear. However, it was music of a sort, and everyone was pleased with it. Perhaps awakened by the sound, the dogs of the village had now started an angry chorus of barking; this was particularly audible to the photographer who sat at the entrance, and it bothered him. He rose and moved over to an empty crate alongside the opposite wall, resting his head against a rough-hewn pole that was one of the supports of the roof. A foot or so above his head there was a strange object dangling from a nail. Now and then he rolled his eyes upward and studied it.

All at once he jumped up and began violently to brush the back of his neck and head. The pole behind him was swarming with tiny ants, thousands upon thousands of them: someone had hung a small crushed coral snake over the nail, and they had come to eat the flesh. It took him a good while not to feel any more of the insects running over his back; during that time two other individuals had come into the *cantina* (whether from the outside or through the door behind the counter, he had not noticed), and now sat between him and the bar in such a fashion that both of them faced him. The old man looked Nordic, the innocent-looking one-legged boy with him could be Spanish; the old man was telling the boy a humorous story, leaning towards him with great interest, occasionally poking his arm with a forefinger to drive home a point, but the boy was distraughtly making designs in the sand with the tip of his crutch.

The photographer stood up; he had never before had such an effect from two drinks. A very peculiar sensation, he said to himself. 'Very peculiar,' he repeated aloud under his breath as he started towards the bar to order another. It was not that he felt drunk so much as that he had become someone who was not he, someone for whom the act of living was a thing so different from what he had imagined it could be, that he was left stranded in a region of sensation far from any he had heretofore known. It was not unpleasant; it was merely undefinable. '*Dispénseme*,' he said to a tall Negro in pink and white striped BVDs, and he handed his empty glass to the fat man. He wanted to see what went into a *cumbiamba*, but the barman did everything quickly beneath the counter and handed him back the glass, brimming with the slightly frothy mixture. He took a good swallow of it and set it down, turning a little to his right as he did so. Standing beside him was the Indian soldier, his cap at an angle atop a pre-Colombian face. Why does the army put such big visors on them? he wondered.

He saw that the soldier was about to speak. Whatever he says is going to turn out to be an insult, he warned himself, in the hope that this would help him to avoid possible anger later.

'Do you like this place?' the soldier said, his voice was silken.

'*Es simpático*. Yes, I like it'

'Why?' The dogs outside had come nearer; he could hear their yapping now above the laughter.

'Can you tell me why they hung that dead snake on the wall there?' he found himself asking, and supposed it was to change the subject. But the soldier was going to be even more boring than he had feared. 'I asked you why you like this *cantina*,' he insisted.

'And I told you it was *simpático*. Isn't that enough?'

The soldier tilted his head back and looked down his nose.

'Far from being enough,' he replied, his manner pedantic, his expression infuriating.

The photographer returned to his drink, picked it up, slowly finished it off. Then he pulled out his cigarettes and offered one to the other. With exaggerated deliberateness the soldier reached for the cigarette, took it, and began to tap it on the counter. The man playing the guitar at last had started to sing in a small falsetto voice along with it, but most of the words were in a dialect the photographer could not understand. When the cigarettes were lighted, he found himself wondering who had lighted them – he or the soldier.

'Just where did you come from?' asked the soldier.

He was not bothering to answer, but the soldier misunderstood even this. 'I can see you're inventing something,' he said, 'and I don't want to hear it.'

The photographer, disgusted, exclaimed: 'Aaah!' and ordered another *cumbiamba*. This most recent one had done something extraordinary to him: he felt that he had become very precise, thin and hard, an object made of enamel or some similar material, something other than a living being, but intensely conscious all the same. Four ought to do the trick, he thought.

The empty glass was in his hand, the fat barman was staring at him, and at that point he had not the slightest idea whether he had already drunk the fourth one or whether it was still the moment just after he had ordered it. He felt himself laughing, but he could not hear whether any sound was coming out or not. The mangled snake, seething with ants, had upset him a little; recognizing it, he had then been made aware of its smell, which he was not sure he had escaped even now. Here at the bar the kerosene lamp smoked heavily; its strong fumes choked him. '*Gracias a Dios*,' he confided to the barman, handing him the glass.

The old man who had been sitting on the crate behind them rose and came vaguely towards the bar. 'Where did this come from?' said the photographer, laughing apologetically, looking at the full glass in his hand. The frenzied dogs out in the clearing yapped and howled, an exasperating sound. '*Qué tienen esos perros?*' he demanded of the soldier.

The old man had stopped beside them. 'Say, Jack, I don't

mean to butt in or anything,' he began. He was bald, sunburned; he wore a fishnet shirt. The furrows between his ribs showed as parallel shadows, and irregular tufts of grey hair waved out from his chest between the meshes of the shirt. He stretched his lips in a smile, showing naked white gums. The soldier's stance became over-nonchalant; he stared at the newcomer, open hatred suddenly in his eyes, and gently blew the smoke from his cigarette into the old man's face.

'You from Milwaukee? Siddown.'

'In a little while, thanks,' said the photographer.

'A little while?' the old man echoed incredulously, running his hand over the top of his head. Then he called out in Spanish to the one-legged boy. The photographer was thinking: This is not going to work out right, at all. It's just not going to work out. He wished the Negro would stop singing and the dogs would stop barking. He looked at the glass in his hand, full of what looked like soapsuds. Someone tapped him on the shoulder. 'Say, Bud, lemme give you a little advice.' The old man again. 'There's money in this country if you know where to look. But the guy that finds it is the guy that sticks to his own kind, if you know what I mean.' He put his face nearer and lowered his voice. Three skeletal fingers touched the photographer's arm. 'You take it from me, from one white man to another. I'm tellin' you!' The three fingers, dark with tobacco stain, lifted themselves, trembled, and dropped back. 'These guys all mean trouble from the word go.'

The boy having both gathered up his crutch and managed to rise from where he had been sitting, had now arrived at the bar. 'Take a look at this, Jack,' the old man said. 'Show him,' he told the boy in Spanish, and the boy, leaning on his crutch, bent over and rolled up the right leg of his ragged khaki shorts until he had exposed the stump of his amputated leg. It was not far below the groin; the scar tissue had puckered and wrinkled curiously in countless tiny convolutions. 'See?' cried the old man. 'Two hundred and sixty tons of bananas went over that. Feel it.'

'You feel it,' said the photographer, wondering how it was possible for him to go on standing and talking exactly as if he were a person like the rest of them. (Could it be that what had happened to him did not show?) He turned his head and looked towards the entrance. The mulatto girl was vomiting just outside. With a cry the barman rushed across and furiously pushed her further away, out into the clearing. When he came back in he was theatrically holding his nose. 'That prostitute ape!' he yelled. 'In another minute we'd have had the dogs inside here.'

The boy was still looking expectantly at the old man, to see if it was time to lower his trouser leg. 'You think he got a centavo from them?' said the old man sadly. 'Hah!'

The photographer had begun to suspect that something had gone very wrong inside him. He felt sick, but since he was no longer a living creature he could not conceive it in those terms. He had shut his eyes and put his hand over his face. 'It's going around backwards,' he said. The undrunk *cumbiamba* was in his other hand.

Saying the sentence had made it more true. It was definitely going around backwards. The important thing was to remember that he was alone here and that this was a real place with real people in it. He could feel how dangerously easy it would be to go along with the messages given him by his senses, and dismiss the whole thing as a nightmare in the secret belief that when the breaking-point came he could somehow manage to escape by waking himself up. A little unsteadily he set his drink down on the counter. An argument which had arisen a while ago between the Indian soldier and his sad companion had now reached its noisy stage, with the companion attempting to drag the soldier away from the bar against his will, and the soldier, his two booted legs firmly apart, breathing rapidly, noisily in his resistance. Suddenly there was a small, shining knife in his right hand, and his face assumed the look of a little boy about to burst into tears. The old man quickly moved around to the photographer's other side. 'That guy's bad news in any language,' he muttered, gesturing nervously to the boy with the crutch as he bade him move out of the way.

The photographer was saying to himself: If I can hold out. If I can only hold out. The whole place was slipping away from him, downward and outward; the guitar strummed and the dogs barked, the soldier flashed his knife and pouted, the old American talked about caves with buried emeralds only six days up the Tupurú, the lamp grew redder and more smoke came out of it. He understood nothing except that he must stay there and suffer; to try to escape would be fatal. The soldier's face was very near his own now, breathing black tobacco smoke at him. Languorously, with an insane natural coquetry, he made his long lashes tremble as he asked: 'Why have you not offered me a *copita?* All night I have been waiting for you to invite me.' The hand holding the knife hung listlessly at his side; the photographer thought of a sleeping baby still clutching its rattle.

'*Sí quieres.* . . . *Qué tomas?*' he murmured, reflecting that his shoes should be in his hand and were not; then where were they? Someone had brought a large spider monkey into the *cantina* and was forcing it to dance to the guitar's syncopations, making it stand upright by holding its two front paws. With an air of distraught gravity it stepped about, peering this way and that, grimacing nervously at the loud peals of laughter that came from those at the bar watching its antics. The dogs, having noticed its arrival, had rushed to the very entrance of the *cantina*, where they braced themselves to shriek and snap with determined fury.

The soldier's drink had been bought and paid for, but he was not drinking it. He was leaning far back against the bar, reclining on his elbow almost as though he were in bed, his eyes simple black slits, whispering: 'You don't like it here. You want to go, *verdad?* But you are afraid to go.'

In spite of the constant sliding away, everything had remained just as it was. It would have been better if he could have sat down. Oh, God, he asked himself. Am I going to be able to stand this?

'Why are you afraid to go?' pursued the other tenderly, smiling so that the photographer could admire his small, perfect teeth. The photographer laughed silently, did not reply.

The face of the soldier, ovoid, honey-coloured, so near to his, moved now with consummate smoothness into another face, that of a general. ('*Sí, mi general,*' with stiff *bigotes* sprouting from beneath the nostrils, almond eyes, black, deadly with a delicate lust, the uniform svelte, plaited steel riding crop in hand, sharpened spurs shining by the ankle-bone. '*Bien, mi general.*' Lying on the hot barrack mattress, *tarde tras tarde*, the soldier had dreamed of being the general. Which mountain village had he said he was from? How long had he been talking?)

'... and that day alone they killed forty-one pigs before my eyes. There in the corral. *Me hizo algo; no sé....*' His smile was apologetic, intimate; he lowered his eyes imperceptibly, made the effort and raised them again to look at the photographer in such a way that, since they were wider than before, they glistened. 'I never forgot it; I don't know why.'

Between them the gold-toothed girl came sliding, her hands wriggling over her head, her hips circling, her thin voice shouting: '*Ahii! Ahii! El fandango de la Guajira!*' The soldier must have pushed her, for all at once she slapped him. But it was happening very slowly. How could it take the soldier so long to bring up his knife, and as he raised his hand, how could the stupid girl wait that way before screaming and ducking aside? Even so, the blade caught her only on the arm; she was in the middle of the floor, kneeling on the sand, moaning: 'He cut me! Oh, God! He cut me!' And because the man who had been dancing with the spider monkey let go of it to get as quickly as all the others to the bar, the beast toddled over to the girl and distractedly wrapped one long hairy arm around her neck. But then the photographer was being roughly jostled, his bare feet were being stepped on as everyone tried to get at the soldier and disarm him. (A demon mask shiny with venom, a voice of barbed wire that rasped: '*Os mato a todos! A todos!*')

It was exactly nineteen steps from the place where he had stood to the trunk of a small papaya tree in front of the entrance. The tree was not very strong; it swayed slightly as he leaned against it. The dogs were yelping now from inside the *cantina*. Here the air was sweet and almost cool; the faintest glimmer of morning was in the sky and water behind the landing. I must start to walk, he told himself; it seemed important to believe it. The shouts and screams inside the *cantina* were growing in volume, and people were beginning to call to one another from the doors of their huts. The landing platform was empty – just boards and no railing. Shuffling along with great care because he was not used to going barefoot, he followed what he thought was the path he had taken earlier, through the undergrowth back down to the river's edge, and there was the punt, mud-beached in the mangroves.

It was easy to get in, easy to untie the rope, and easy (for the level of the water had risen considerably since the craft had been left) to pry it loose from the shelf of mud where it rested. But once he was floating among the now nearly visible trunks and branches, bumping against them and being spun to face first the dark chaotic river-bank and then the wide whitening emptiness of open sky and water, he understood dimly that it was not going to be possible to pole his way back to the beach whence he had come, since the tide was still coming in. It was a comforting thought, he decided, because it meant that everything was going ahead instead of backwards. A minute later he was floating quietly by the base of the landing: people were running around the clearing. Quickly he lay down flat on the bottom of the punt, and there he stayed, looking straight up at the grey sky, hoping in this way to remain invisible until he had been carried out of sight, beyond Tapiama.

It was going to be one of those stillborn tropical days, when there would be no sun, no wind, no clouds – because the entire sky was enfolded in one vast suffocating blanket of cloud – when nothing at all would happen save that hourly it would grow hotter until an approximate dusk came along. Already the eastern side of the sky was the hot side, arching above the flatness of the swamp-land. The punt scarcely moved now, the channel having broadened into this wide marshy lake. The photographer lay still and groaned. Little by little the fear that someone might see him gave way to the hope that what current there was might propel the craft in the direction of the shore rather than out towards the wilderness of water and tiny islands; sometimes, even though suffering be implicit in it, contact with others is preferable to the terror of solitude and the unknown. He laid an arm over his eyes to shield them from the corrosive grey light that beat down upon him from the spaces above. The other hand lay in the ashes of last night's fire. And he floated in utter silence on the calm bosom of the lagoon, not stirring as the morning hours moved along, but growing increasingly conscious of the infernal seething of the *cumbiambas* in his brain, a seething which expressed itself as a senseless nightmare imposed from without, in the face of which he could only be totally passive. It was an invisible spectacle whose painful logic he followed with the entire fibre of his being, without, however, once being given a clear vision of what agonizing destinies were at stake.

Some time towards mid-morning the punt grazed a submerged root and was swung into an eddyless pool in the shelter of the vegetation near the shore. Here fierce flies stung him, and from among the leaves high above, a talking bird remarked casually, over and over again: 'Idigaraga. Idigaraga. Idigaraga.'

It was no particular consolation to him, so intent was he on the obscure drama being enacted within him, to hear human voices presently, or to feel the craft seized by the hands of someone splashing in the water alongside. Only when several people had climbed in and crouched chattering around him did he move his arm and squint up at them. Five young men, all of whom looked remarkably alike, surrounded him. Water dripped down upon him from their naked bodies. He shut his eyes again: it was too unlikely a scene. During this time one of them dived overboard, was gone for a short while, and returned with a green coconut whose top he had sliced off. He began to let the water dribble into the photographer's face, whereupon the photographer partially sat up and drank the rest of it. In a minute he looked around at them again, and said: 'Are you brothers?'

'*Sí, si,*' they chorused. This was for some reason a consolation. '*Hermanos,*' he sighed, sliding down into the ashes again. Then he added desperately, hoping they could still hear him: 'Please take me to Rio Martillo.'

It had been a brief interlude of clarity. Now they poled the punt back out under the hot sky, letting him lie there and moan as he liked. At one point he felt he must try to explain that he would give them each seventy-five centavos for their trouble, but they giggled and pushed him back down.

'My shoes!' he cried.

'There are no shoes,' they told him. 'Lie still.'

'And when we get to the beach,' he panted, seizing a brown ankle beside his face, 'how will you get me to Rio Martillo?'

'We are not going to any beach,' they replied. 'We go through the swamp and the canal.'

He lay still a while, trying to disassociate himself from the irrational ideas boiling up in his head. 'Is this the way to Rio Martillo?' he demanded, thrusting himself up a little and gasping, trying to see beyond the enclosing thicket of brown legs and arms, and feeling a deep unreasoned shame at having once again accepted defeat.

They laughed, pushed him gently down to the floor, and went on rhythmically poling the craft eastward. 'The factory chimney,' they said to one another, pointing into the distance.

His mind took him back to the quiet region by the river-bank where the small bird had spoken, high up in the trees, and he heard again the ridiculous conversational tone. 'Idigaraga,' he said aloud, imitating perfectly its voice and intonation.

There was an explosion of mirth around him. One of the youths took his arm, shook it lightly. 'You know that bird?' he said. 'It is a very comic bird. It goes to the nests of other birds and wants to sit there, and when the other birds fight with it and drive it away, it sits down in the same tree there and says: "Idigaraga." That means: "*Iri garagua, nadie me quiere*, nobody likes me." And it says it over and over, until they make it go further away so they can't hear it any more. You said it just right. Say it again.'

'*Sí, sí,*' the others agreed, '*otra vez!*'

The photographer had no intention of saying it again. His shame at having accepted defeat already troubled him less. It was hard in his present condition to fit the bird correctly into the pattern, but he knew it had to be done.

When the Compañía Azucarera Riomartillense blew a long blast on its whistle to announce the advent of noon, the sound hovered for an instant over the empty swamp-land like an invisible trail of smoke. '*Las doce,*' said one of the brothers. A great black and gold dragonfly came skimming across the water and lighted on the photographer's bare foot. After raising and lowering its wings twice, it was away again on its crooked course, curving and swooping over the lagoon towards Tapiama.

By the Water

The melting snow dripped from the balconies. People hurried through the little street that always smelled of frying fish. Now and then a stork swooped low, dragging his sticklike legs below him. The small gramophones scraped day and night behind the walls of the shop where young Amar worked and lived. There were few spots in the city where the snow was ever cleared away, and this was not one of them. So it gathered all through the winter months, piling up in front of the shop doors.

But now it was late winter; the sun was warmer. Spring was on the way, to confuse the heart and melt the snow. Amar, being alone in the world, decided it was time to visit a neighbouring city where his father had once told him some cousins lived.

Early in the morning he went to the bus station. It was still dark, and the empty bus came in while he was drinking hot coffee. The road wound through the mountains all the way.

When he arrived in the other city it was already dark. Here the snow was even deeper in the streets, and it was colder. Because he had not wanted to, Amar had not foreseen this, and it annoyed him to be forced to wrap his burnous closely about him as he left the bus station. It was an unfriendly town; he could tell that immediately. Men walked with their heads bent forward, and if they brushed against a passer-by they did not so much as look up. Excepting the principal street, which had an arc-light every few metres, there seemed to be no other illumination, and the alleys that led off on either side lay in utter blackness; the white-clad figures that turned into them disappeared straightway.

150

'A bad town,' said Amar under his breath. He felt proud to be coming from a better and larger city, but his pleasure was mingled with anxiety about the night to be passed in this inimical place. He abandoned the idea of trying to find his cousins before morning, and set about looking for a *fondouk* or a bath where he might sleep until daybreak.

Only a short distance ahead the street-lighting system terminated. Beyond, the street appeared to descend sharply and lose itself in darkness. The snow was uniformly deep here, and not cleared away in patches as it had been nearer the bus station. He puckered his lips and blew his breath ahead of him in little clouds of steam. As he passed over into the unlighted district he heard a few languid notes being strummed on an oud. The music came from a doorway on his left. He paused and listened. Someone approached the doorway from the other direction and inquired, apparently of the man with the oud, if it was 'too late'.

'No,' the musician answered, and he played several more notes.

Amar went over to the door.

'Is there still time?' he said.

'Yes.'

He stepped inside the door. There was no light, but he could feel warm air blowing upon his face from the corridor to the right. He walked ahead, letting his hand run along the damp wall beside him. Soon he came into a large dimly lit room with a tile floor. Here and there, at various angles, figures lay asleep, wrapped in grey blankets. In a far corner a group of men, partially dressed, sat about a burning brazier, drinking tea and talking in low tones. Amar slowly approached them, taking care not to step on the sleepers.

The air was oppressively warm and moist.

'Where is the bath?' said Amar.

'Down there,' answered one of the men in the group, without even looking up. He indicated the dark corner to his left. And, indeed, now that Amar considered it, it seemed to him that a warm current of air came up from that part of the room. He went in the direction of the dark corner, undressed, and leaving his clothes in a neat pile on a piece of straw matting, walked toward the warmth. He was thinking of the misfortune he had encountered in arriving in this town at nightfall, and he wondered if his clothes would be molested during his absence. He wore his money in a leather pouch which hung on a string about his neck. Feeling vaguely of the purse under his chin, he turned around to look once again at his clothing. No one seemed to have noticed him as he undressed. He went on. It would not do to seem too distrustful. He would be embroiled immediately in a quarrel which could only end badly for him.

A little boy rushed out of the darkness toward him, calling: 'Follow me, Sidi, I shall lead you to the bath.' He was extremely dirty and ragged, and looked rather more like a midget than a child. Leading the way, he chattered as they went down the slippery, warm steps in the dark. 'You will call for Brahim when you want your tea? You're a stranger. You have much money. . . .'

Amar cut him short. 'You'll get your coins when you come to wake me in the morning. Not tonight.'

'But, Sidi! I'm not allowed in the big room. I stay in the doorway and show gentlemen down to the bath. Then I go back to the doorway. I can't wake you.'

'I'll sleep near the doorway. It's warmer there, in any case.'

'Lazrag will be angry and terrible things will happen. I'll never get home again, or if I do I might be a bird so my parents will not know me. That's what Lazrag does when he gets angry.'

'Lazrag?'

'It is his place here. You'll see him. He never goes out. If he did the sun would burn him in one second, like a straw in the fire. He would fall down in the street burned black the minute he stepped out of the door. He was born down here in the grotto.'

Amar was not paying strict attention to the boy's babble. They were descending a wet stone ramp, putting one foot before the other slowly in the dark, and feeling the rough wall carefully as they went. There was the sound of splashing water and voices ahead.

'This is a strange *hammam*,' said Amar. 'Is there a pool full of water?'

'A pool! You've never heard of Lazrag's grotto? It goes on

for ever, and it's made of deep warm water.'

As the boy spoke, they came out on to a stone balcony a few metres above the beginning of a very large pool, lighted beneath where they stood by two bare electric bulbs, and stretching away through the dimness into utter dark beyond. Parts of the roof hung down, Like grey icicles, thought Amar, as he looked about in wonder. But it was very warm down here. A slight pall of steam lay above the surface of the water, rising constantly in wisps toward the rocky ceiling. A man dripping with water ran past them and dived in. Several more were swimming about in the brighter region near the lights, never straying beyond into the gloom. The plunging and shouting echoed violently beneath the low ceiling.

Amar was not a good swimmer. He turned to ask the boy: 'Is it deep?' but he had already disappeared back up the ramp. He stepped backward and leaned against the rock wall. There was a low chair to his right, and in the murky light it seemed to him that a small figure was close beside it. He watched the bathers for a few minutes. Those standing at the edge of the water soaped themselves assiduously; those in the water swam to and fro in a short radius below the lights. Suddenly a deep voice spoke close beside him. He looked down as he heard it say: 'Who are you?'

The creature's head was large; its body was small and it had no legs or arms. The lower part of the trunk ended in two flipper-like pieces of flesh. From the shoulders grew short pincers. It was a man, and it was looking up at him from the floor where it rested.

'Who are you?' it said again, and its tone was unmistakably hostile.

Amar hesitated. 'I came to bathe and sleep,' he said at last.

'Who gave you permission?'

'The man at the entrance.'

'Get out. I don't know you.'

Amar was filled with anger. He looked down with scorn at the little being, and stepped away from it to join the men washing themselves by the water's edge. But more swiftly than he moved, it managed to throw itself along the floor until it was in front of him, when it raised itself again and spoke.

'You think you can bathe when I tell you to get out?' It laughed shortly, a thin sound, but deep in pitch. Then it moved closer and pushed its head against Amar's legs. He drew back his foot and kicked the head, not very hard, but with enough firmness to send the body off balance. The thing rolled over in silence, making efforts with its neck to keep from reaching the edge of the platform. The men all looked up. An expression of fear was on their faces. As the little creature went over the edge it yelled. The splash was like that of a large stone. Two men already in the water swam quickly to the spot. The others started up after Amar, shouting: 'He hit Lazrag!'

Bewildered and frightened, Amar turned and ran back to the ramp. In the blackness he stumbled upward. Part of the wall scraped his bare thigh. The voices behind him grew louder and more excited.

He reached the room where he had left his clothing. Nothing had changed. The men still sat by the brazier talking. Quickly he snatched the pile of garments, and struggling into his burnous, he ran to the door that led into the street, the rest of his clothes tucked under his arm. The man in the doorway with the oud looked at him with a startled face and called after him. Amar ran up the street barelegged toward the centre of the town. He wanted to be where there were some bright lights. The few people walking in the street paid him no attention. When he got to the bus station it was closed. He went into a small park opposite, where the iron bandstand stood deep in snow. There on a cold stone bench he sat and dressed himself as unostentatiously as possible, using his burnous as a screen. He was shivering, reflecting bitterly upon his poor luck, and wishing he had not left his own town, when a small figure approached him in the half-light.

'Sidi,' it said, 'come with me. Lazrag is hunting for you.'

'Where to?' said Amar, recognizing the urchin from the bath.

'My grandfather's.'

The boy began to run, motioning to him to follow. They went through alleys and tunnels, into the most congested part of the town. The boy did not bother to look back, but

Amar did. They finally paused before a small door at the side of a narrow passageway. The boy knocked vigorously. From within came a cracked voice calling: '*Chkoun?*'

'*Annah!* Brahim!' cried the boy.

With great deliberation the old man swung the door open and stood looking at Amar.

'Come in,' he finally said; and shutting the door behind them he led them through the courtyard filled with goats into an inner room where a feeble light was flickering. He peered sternly into Amar's face.

'He wants to stay here tonight,' explained the boy.

'Does he think this is a *fondouk?*'

'He has money,' said Brahim hopefully.

'Money!' the old man cried with scorn. 'That's what you learn in the *hammam!* How to steal money! How to take money from men's purses! Now you bring them here! What do you want me to do? Kill him and get his purse for you? Is he too clever for you? You can't get it by yourself? Is that it?' The old man's voice had risen to a scream and he gestured in his mounting excitement. He sat down on a cushion with difficulty and was silent a moment.

'Money,' he said again, finally. 'Let him go to a *fondouk* or a bath. Why aren't you at the *hammam?*' He looked suspiciously at his grandson.

The boy clutched at his friend's sleeve. 'Come,' he said, pulling him out into the courtyard.

'Take him to the *hammam!*' yelled the old man. 'Let him spend his money there!'

Together they went back into the dark streets.

'Lazrag is looking for you,' said the boy. 'Twenty men will be going through the town to catch you and take you back to him. He is very angry and he will change you into a bird.'

'Where are we going now?' asked Amar gruffly. He was cold and very tired, and although he did not really believe the boy's story, he wished he were out of the unfriendly town.

'We must walk as far as we can from here. All night. In the morning we'll be far away in the mountains, and they won't find us. We can go to your city.'

Amar did not answer. He was pleased that the boy wanted

to stay with him, but he did not think it fitting to say so. They followed one crooked street downhill until all the houses had been left behind and they were in the open country. The path led down a narrow valley presently, and joined the highway at one end of a small bridge. Here the snow was packed down by the passage of vehicles, and they found it much easier to walk along.

When they had been going down the road for perhaps an hour in the increasing cold, a great truck came rolling by. It stopped just ahead and the driver, an Arab, offered them a ride on top. They climbed up and made a nest of some empty sacks. The boy was very happy to be rushing through the air in the dark night. Mountains and stars whirled by above his head and the truck made a powerful roaring noise as it travelled along the empty highway.

'Lazrag has found us and changed us both into birds,' he cried when he could no longer keep his delight to himself. 'No one will ever know us again.'

Amar grunted and went to sleep. But the boy watched the sky and the trees and the cliffs for a long time before he closed his eyes.

Some time before morning the truck stopped by a spring for water.

In the stillness the boy awoke. A cock crowed in the distance, and then he heard the driver pouring water. The cock crowed again, a sad, thin arc of sound away in the cold murk of the plain. It was not yet dawn. He buried himself deeper in the pile of sacks and rags, and felt the warmth of Amar as he slept.

When daylight came they were in another part of the land. There was no snow. Instead, the almond trees were in flower on the hillsides as they sped past. The road went on unwinding as it dropped lower and lower, until suddenly it came out of the hills upon a spot below which lay a great glittering emptiness. Amar and the boy watched it and said to each other that it must be the sea, shining in the morning light.

The spring wind pushed the foam from the waves along the beach; it rippled Amar's and the boy's garments landward as they walked by the edge of the water. Finally they found a sheltered spot between rocks, and undressed, leaving the clothes on the sand. The boy was afraid to go into the water, and found enough excitement in letting the waves break about his legs, but Amar tried to drag him out further.

'No, no!'

'Come,' Amar urged him.

Amar looked down. Approaching him sideways was an enormous crab which had crawled out from a dark place in the rocks. He leaped back in terror, lost his balance, and fell heavily, striking his head against one of the great boulders. The boy stood perfectly still watching the animal make its cautious way toward Amar through the tips of the breaking waves. Amar lay without moving, rivulets of water and sand running down his face. As the crab reached his feet, the boy bounded into the air, and in a voice made hoarse by desperation, screamed: 'Lazrag!'

The crab scuttled swiftly behind the rock and disappeared. The boy's face became radiant. He rushed to Amar, lifted his head above a newly breaking wave, and slapped his cheeks excitedly.

'Amar! I made him go away!' he shouted. 'I saved you!'

If he did not move, the pain was not too great. So Amar lay still, feeling the warm sunlight, the soft water washing over him, and the cool, sweet wind that came in from the sea. He also felt the boy trembling in his effort to hold his head above the waves, and he heard him saying many times over: 'I saved you, Amar.'

After a long time he answered: 'Yes.'

A Thousand Days for
Mokhtar

Mokhtar lived in a room not far from his shop, overlooking
the sea. There was a tiny window in the wall above his
sleeping-mattress, through which, if he stood on tiptoe, he
could see the waves pounding against the rocks of the
breakwater far below. The sound came up, too, especially on
nights when the Casbah was wrapped in rain and its narrow
streets served only for the passage of unexpected gusts of
wind. On these nights the sound of the waves was all around,
even though he kept the window shut. Throughout the year
there were many such nights, and it was precisely at such
times that he did not feel like going home to be alone in his
little room. He had been by himself ten years now, ever since
his wife had died; his solitude never weighed on him when
the weather was clear and the stars shone in the sky. But a
rainy night put him in mind of the happy hours of his life,
when in just such nocturnal wind and storm he and his
great-eyed bride would pull the heavy blinds shut and live
quietly in each other's company until dawn. These things he
could not think about; he would go to the Café Ghazel and
play dominoes hour after hour with anyone who came along,
rather than return to his room.

Little by little the other men who sat regularly in the café
had come to count on Mokhtar's appearance. 'It's beginning
to rain: Si Mokhtar will be along soon. Save him the mat
next to you.' And he never disappointed them. He was
pleasant and quiet; the latter quality made him a welcome
addition to a game, since the café's habitués considered each

other far too talkative.

Sitting in the Café Ghazel tonight Mokhtar was un-accountably uneasy. He was disturbed by the bonelike sound of the dominoes as they were shuffled on the tables. The metallic scraping of the old phonograph in the inner room bothered him, and he looked up with an unreasoning annoyance at each new arrival who came in through the door, heralded by blasts of wet wind. Often he glanced out the window beside him at the vast blackness of the sea lying below at the foot of the city. On the other side of the glass, just at the edge of the cliff, a few tall stalks of bamboo caught the light from inside, stood out white against the blackness beyond, bending painfully before the gale.

'They'll break,' murmured Mokhtar.

'What?' said Mohammed Slaoui.

Mokhtar laughed, but said nothing. As the evening continued, his discomfort increased. In the inner room they had stopped the phonograph and were singing a strident song. Some of the men around him joined in the noise. He could no longer hear the wind. As that round of dominoes came to an end, he rose precipitately and said: 'Good-night', not caring how strange his sudden departure might seem to the others.

Outside in the street it was scarcely raining at all, but the wind raged upward from the shore below, bringing with it the bloodlike smell of the sea; the crashing waves seemed very near, almost at his feet. He looked down as he walked along. At each mound of garbage there were cats; they ran across in front of him constantly from one pile to another. As Mokhtar reached his door and pulled out his key, he had the feeling that he was about to perform an irrevocable act, that stepping inside would be a gesture of finality.

What is happening? he asked himself. Am I going to die? He would not be afraid of that; still, he would like to know it a few moments in advance, if possible. He flexed his arms and legs before opening the door: there was no pain anywhere, everything appeared to be in good condition. It's my head, he decided. But his head felt clear, his thoughts moved forward in orderly fashion. Nevertheless, these discoveries did not reassure him; he knew something was wrong. He bolted the door behind him and began to mount the stairs in the dark. More clearly than anything else at the moment he sensed that this conviction of having entered into a new region of his life was only in the nature of a warning. 'Don't go on,' he was being told. Doing what? he asked himself as he undressed. He had no secrets, no involvements, no plans for the future, no responsibilities. He merely lived. He could not heed the warning because he could not understand it. And yet there was no doubt that it was there in his room, and it made itself most strongly felt when he lay down. The wind shook the blinds. The rain had begun to fall again; it showered violently on the panes of glass over the corridor, and rattled down the drain-pipe from the roof. And the unappeased roaring of the waves went on, down at the base of the ramparts. He considered the sadness, the coldness of the damp blanket; he touched the straw-covered wall with his finger. In the black night he groaned: 'Al-lah!' and fell asleep.

But even in sleep he went on worrying; his dreams were a chaotic, relentless continuation of his waking state. The same accent of implicit warning was present in the sequences of streets and shops which unrolled before his eyes. He was at the entrance to the public market. A great many people were inside, where they had gone to get out of the rain. Although it was mid-morning, the day was so dark that all the stalls were blazing with electric lights. If only she could have seen this, he said to himself, thinking of how much pleasure it would have given his wife. Poor girl, in her day it was always dark here. And Mokhtar wondered if really he had the right to go on living and watching the world change, without her. Each month the world had changed a little more, had gone a little further away from what it had been when she had known it.

Also, since she is not here to eat it, what am I doing buying meat? He was standing before the stall of his friend Abdallah ben Bouchta, looking at the cuts that were displayed on the slab of white marble in front of him. And all at once he was embroiled in a quarrel with Bouchta. He felt himself seizing the old man by the throat; he felt his fingers pressing with increasing force: he was choking Bouchta and he was glad to be doing it. The violence of the act was a fulfilment and a relief. Bouchta's face grew black, he fell, and his glazed eyes stared like the eyes in a sheep's head served on a platter for the feast of Aïd el Kébir.

Mokhtar awoke, horrified. The wind was still blowing, carrying with it, above the town, wisps of the voice of the muezzin who at that moment was calling from the Jaamâa es Seghira. But the warnings had ceased, and this was comforting enough to make more sleep possible.

The morning was grey and cheerless. Mokhtar rose at the usual hour, made his daily visit to the great mosque for a few moments of prayer and a thorough wash, and proceeded through the rain to his shop. There were few people in the streets. The memory of his dream weighed upon him, saddening him even more than the prospect of a day of infrequent sales. As the morning progressed he thought often of his old friend; he was consumed with the desire to pass by the market, just to assure himself that Bouchta was there as always. There was no reason why he should not be, but once Mokhtar had seen him with his own eyes he would be content.

A little before noon he boarded up the front of his shop and set out for the market. When his eyes became accustomed to the dim inner light of the building, the first person he saw was Bouchta standing behind the counter in his stall, chopping and slicing the meat the same as any other day. Feeling immensely relieved, Mokhtar wandered over to the counter and spoke to him. Perhaps the note of excessive cordiality in his voice surprised Bouchta, for he glanced up with a startled expression in his face, and seeing Mokhtar, said shortly: '*Sbalkheir.*' Then he resumed hacking at a piece of meat for a customer. His rather unfriendly look was lost on Mokhtar, who was so pleased to see him there that he was momentarily unable to perceive anything but that one fact. However, when Bouchta, on completing the sale, turned to him, and said abruptly: 'I'm busy this morning,' Mokhtar stared at him, and again felt his fear stir within him.

'Yes, Sidi?' he said pleasantly.

Bouchta glared. 'Twenty-two douro would be a more welcome offering than your foolish smile,' he said.

Mokhtar looked confused. 'Twenty-two douro, Sidi?'

'Yes. The twenty-two douro you never paid me for the lamb's head at last Aïd el Kébir.'

Mokhtar felt the blood leap upward in him like a fire. 'I paid you for that the following month.'

'*Abaden!* Never!' cried Bouchta excitedly. 'I have eyes and a head too! I remember what happens! You can't take advantage of me the way you did of poor old Tahiri. I'm not that old yet!' And he began to call out unpleasant epithets, brandishing his cleaver.

People had stopped in their tracks and were following the conversation with interest. As Mokhtar's anger mounted, he suddenly heard, among the names that Bouchta was calling him, one which offended him more than the rest. He reached across the counter and seized Bouchta's djellaba in his two hands, pulling on the heavy woollen fabric until it seemed that it would surely be ripped off the old man's back.

'Let go of me!' shouted Bouchta. The people were crowding in to see whatever violence might result. 'Let go of me!' he kept screaming, his face growing steadily redder.

At this point the scene was so much like his dream that Mokhtar, even while he was enjoying his own anger and the sight of Bouchta as he became the victim of such a senseless rage, was suddenly very much frightened. He let go of the djellaba with one hand, and turning to the onlookers said loudly: 'Last night I dreamed that I came here and killed this man, who is my friend. I do not want to kill him. I am not going to kill him. Look carefully. I am not hurting him.'

Bouchta's fury was reaching grotesque proportions. With one hand he was trying to pry Mokhtar's fingers from his garment, and with the other, which held the cleaver, he was making crazy gyrations in the air. All the while he jumped quickly up and down, crying: 'Let go! Let go! *Khalli!*'

At any moment he is going to hit me with the cleaver, thought Mokhtar, and so he seized the wrist that held it, pulling Bouchta against the counter. For a moment they struggled and panted, while the slabs of meat slid about under their arms and fell heavily on to the wet floor. Bouchta was strong, but he was old. Suddenly he relaxed his grasp on the cleaver and Mokhtar felt his muscles cease to push. The crowd murmured. Mokhtar let go of both the wrist and the djellaba, and looked up. Bouchta's face was an impossible colour, like the sides of meat that hung behind him. His mouth opened and his head slowly tilted upward as if he were looking at the ceiling of the market. Then, as if someone had pushed him from behind, he fell forward on to the marble counter and lay still, his nose in a shallow puddle of pinkish water. Mokhtar knew he was dead, and he was a little triumphant as he shouted to everyone: 'I dreamed it! I dreamed it! I told you! Did I kill him? Did I touch him? You saw!' The crowd agreed, nodding.

'Get the police!' cried Mokhtar. 'I want everyone to be my witness.' A few people moved away quietly, not wishing to be involved. But most of them stayed, quite ready to give the authorities their version of the strange phenomenon.

In court the Qadi proved to be unsympathetic. Mokhtar was bewildered by his lack of friendliness. The witnesses had told the story exactly as it had happened; obviously they all were convinced of Mokhtar's innocence.

'I have heard from the witnesses what happened in the market,' said the Qadi impatiently, 'and from those same witnesses I know you are an evil man. It is impossible for the mind of an upright man to bring forth an evil dream. Bouchta died as a result of your dream.' And as Mokhtar attempted to interrupt: 'I know what you are going to say, but you are a fool, Mokhtar. You blame the wind, the night, your long solitude. Good. For a thousand days in our prison here you will not hear the wind, you will not know whether it is night or day, and you will never lack the companionship of your fellow prisoners.'

The Qadi's sentence shocked the inhabitants of the town, who found it of an unprecedented severity. But Mokhtar, once he had been locked up, was persuaded of its wisdom. For one thing, he was not unhappy to be in prison, where each night, when he had begun to dream that he was back in his lonely room, he could awaken to hear on all sides of him the comforting snores of the other prisoners. His mind no longer dwelled upon the earlier happy hours of his life, because the present hours were happy ones as well. And then, the very first day there, he had suddenly remembered with perfect clarity that, although he had intended to do so, he never had paid Bouchta the twenty-two douro for the lamb's head, after all.

A Distant Episode

The September sunsets were at their reddest the week the Professor decided to visit Aïn Tadouirt, which is in the warm country. He came down out of the high, flat region in the evening by bus, with two small overnight bags full of maps, sun lotions and medicines. Ten years ago he had been in the village for three days; long enough, however, to establish a fairly firm friendship with a café-keeper, who had written him several times during the first year after his visit, if never since. 'Hassan Ramani,' the Professor said over and over, as the bus bumped downward through ever warmer layers of air. Now facing the flaming sky in the west, and now facing the sharp mountains, the car followed the dusty trail down the canyons into air which began to smell of other things besides the endless ozone of the heights: orange blossoms, pepper, sun-baked excrement, burning olive oil, rotten fruit. He closed his eyes happily and lived for an instant in a purely olfactory world. The distant past returned – what part of it, he could not decide.

The chauffeur, whose seat the Professor shared, spoke to him without taking his eyes from the road. '*Vous êtes géologue?*'

'A geologist? Ah, no! I'm a linguist.'

'There are no languages here. Only dialects.'

'Exactly. I'm making a survey of variations on Moghrebi.'

The chauffeur was scornful. 'Keep on going south,' he said. 'You'll find some languages you never heard of before.'

As they drove through the town gate, the usual swarm of urchins rose up out of the dust and ran screaming beside the bus. The Professor folded his dark glasses, put them in his

164

pocket; and as soon as the vehicle had come to a standstill he jumped out, pushing his way through the indignant boys who clutched at his luggage in vain, and walked quickly into the Grand Hotel Saharien. Out of its eight rooms there were two available – one facing the market and the other, a smaller and cheaper one, giving on to a tiny yard full of refuse and barrels, where two gazelles wandered about. He took the smaller room, and pouring the entire pitcher of water into the tin basin, began to wash the grit from his face and ears. The afterglow was nearly gone from the sky, and the pinkness in objects was disappearing, almost as he watched. He lit the carbide lamp and winced at its odour.

After dinner the Professor walked slowly through the streets to Hassan Ramani's café, whose back room hung hazardously out above the river. The entrance was very low, and he had to bend down slightly to get in. A man was tending the fire. There was one guest sipping tea. The *qaouaji* tried to make him take a seat at the other table in the front room, but the Professor walked airily ahead into the back room and sat down. The moon was shining through the reed latticework and there was not a sound outside but the occasional distant bark of a dog. He changed tables so he could see the river. It was dry, but there was a pool here and there that reflected the bright night sky. The *qaouaji* came in and wiped off the table.

'Does this café still belong to Hassan Ramani?' he asked him in the Moghrebi he had taken four years to learn.

The man replied in bad French: 'He is deceased.'

'Deceased?' repeated the Professor, without noticing the absurdity of the word. 'Really? When?'

'I don't know,' said the *qaouaji*. 'One tea?'

'Yes. But I don't understand. . . .'

The man was already out of the room, fanning the fire. The Professor sat still, feeling lonely, and arguing with himself that to do so was ridiculous. Soon the *qaouaji* returned with the tea. He paid him and gave him an enormous tip, for which he received a grave bow.

'Tell me,' he said, as the other started away. 'Can one still get those little boxes made from camel udders?'

The man looked angry. 'Sometimes the Reguibat bring in

those things. We do not buy them here.' Then insolently, in Arabic: 'And why a camel-udder box?'

'Because I like them,' retorted the Professor. And then because he was feeling a little exalted, he added, 'I like them so much I want to make a collection of them, and I will pay you ten francs for every one you can get me.'

'*Khamstache*,' said the *qaouaji*, opening his left hand rapidly three times in succession.

'Never. Ten.'

'Not possible. But wait until later and come with me. You can give me what you like. And you will get camel-udder boxes if there are any.'

He went out into the front room, leaving the Professor to drink his tea and listen to the growing chorus of dogs that barked and howled as the moon rose higher into the sky. A group of customers came into the front room and sat talking for an hour or so. When they had left, the *qaouaji* put out the fire and stood in the doorway putting on his burnous. 'Come,' he said.

Outside in the street there was very little movement. The booths were all closed and the only light came from the moon. An occasional pedestrian passed, and grunted a brief greeting to the *qaouaji*.

'Everyone knows you,' said the Professor, to cut the silence between them.

'Yes.'

'I wish everyone knew me,' said the Professor, before he realized how infantile such a remark must sound.

'*No* one knows you,' said his companion gruffly.

They had come to the other side of the town, on the promontory above the desert, and through a great rift in the wall the Professor saw the white endlessness, broken in the foreground by dark spots of oasis. They walked through the opening and followed a winding road between rocks, downward toward the nearest small forest of palms. The Professor thought: He may cut my throat. But his café – he would surely be found out.

'Is it far?' he asked, casually.

'Are you tired?' countered the *qaouaji*.

'They are expecting me back at the Hotel Saharien,' he lied.

'You can't be there and here,' said the *qaouaji*.

The Professor laughed. He wondered if it sounded uneasy to the other. 'Have you owned Ramani's café long?'

'I work there for a friend.' The reply made the Professor more unhappy than he had imagined it would.

'Oh. Will you work tomorrow?'

'That is impossible to say?'

The Professor stumbled on a stone, and fell, scraping his hand. The *qaouaji* said: 'Be careful.'

The sweet black odour of rotten meat hung in the air suddenly.

'Agh!' said the Professor, choking. 'What is it?'

The *qaouaji* had covered his face with his burnous and did not answer. Soon the stench had been left behind. They were on flat ground. Ahead the path was bordered on each side by a high mud wall. There was no breeze and the palms were quite still, but behind the walls was the sound of running water. Also, the odour of human excrement was almost constant as they walked between the walls.

The Professor waited until he thought it seemed logical for him to ask with a certain degree of annoyance: 'But where are we going?'

'Soon,' said the guide, pausing to gather some stones in the ditch. 'Pick up some stones,' he advised. 'Here are bad dogs.'

'Where?' asked the Professor, but he stopped and got three large ones with pointed edges.

They continued very quietly. The walls came to an end and the bright desert lay ahead. Near by was a ruined marabout, with its tiny dome only half standing, and the front wall entirely destroyed. Behind it were clumps of stunted, useless palms. A dog came running crazily toward them on three legs. Not until it got quite close did the Professor hear its steady low growl. The *qaouaji* let fly a large stone at it, striking it square in the muzzle. There was a strange snapping of jaws and the dog ran sideways in another direction, falling blindly against rocks and scrambling haphazardly about like an injured insect.

Turning off the road, they walked across the earth strewn with sharp stones, past the little ruin, through the trees, until they came to a place where the ground dropped abruptly away in front of them.

'It looks like a quarry,' said the Professor, resorting to French for the word 'quarry', whose Arabic equivalent he could not call to mind at the moment. The *qaouaji* did not answer. Instead he stood still and turned his head, as if listening. And indeed, from somewhere down below, but very far below, came the faint sound of a low flute. The *qaouaji* nodded his head slowly several times. Then he said: 'The path begins here. You can see it well all the way. The rock is white and the moon is strong. So you can see well. I am going back now and sleep. It is late. You can give me what you like.'

Standing there at the edge of the abyss which at each moment looked deeper, with the dark face of the *qaouaji* framed in its moonlit burnous close to his own face, the Professor asked himself exactly what he felt. Indignation, curiosity, fear, perhaps, but most of all relief and the hope that this was not a trick, the hope that the *qaouaji* would really leave him alone and turn back without him.

He stepped back a little from the edge, and fumbled in his pocket for a loose note, because he did not want to show his wallet. Fortunately there was a fifty-franc bill there, which he took out and handed to the man. He knew the *qaouaji* was pleased, and so he paid no attention when he heard him saying: 'It is not enough. I have to walk a long way home and there are dogs . . .'

'Thank you and good night,' said the Professor, sitting down with his legs drawn up under him, and lighting a cigarette. He felt almost happy.

'Give me only one cigarette,' pleaded the man.

'Of course,' he said, a bit curtly, and he held up the pack.

The *qaouaji* squatted close beside him. His face was not pleasant to see. What is it? thought the Professor, terrified again, as he held out his lighted cigarette toward him.

The man's eyes were almost closed. It was the most obvious registering of concentrated scheming the Professor had ever seen. When the second cigarette was burning, he ventured to say to the still-squatting Arab: 'What are you thinking about?'

The other drew on his cigarette deliberately, and seemed about to speak. Then his expression changed to one of satisfaction, but he did not speak. A cool wind had risen in the air, and the Professor shivered. The sound of the flute came up from the depths below at intervals, sometimes mingled with the scraping of nearby palm fronds one against the other. These people are not primitives, the Professor found himself saying in his mind.

'Good,' said the *qaouaji*, rising slowly. 'Keep your money. Fifty francs is enough. It is an honour.' Then he went back into French. '*Ti n'as qu'à discendre, to' droit.*' He spat, chuckled (or was the Professor hysterical?), and strode away quickly.

The Professor was in a state of nerves. He lit another cigarette, and found his lips moving automatically. They were saying: 'Is this a situation or a predicament? This is ridiculous.' He sat very still for several minutes, waiting for a sense of reality to come to him. He stretched out on the hard, cold ground and looked up at the moon. It was almost like looking straight at the sun. If he shifted his gaze a little at a time, he could make a string of weaker moons across the sky. 'Incredible,' he whispered. Then he sat up quickly and looked about. There was no guarantee that the *qaouaji* really had gone back to town. He got to his feet and looked over the edge of the precipice. In the moonlight the bottom seemed miles away. And there was nothing to give it scale; not a tree, not a house, not a person. . . . He listened for the flute, and heard only the wind going by his ears. A sudden violent desire to run back to the road seized him, and he turned and looked in the direction the *qaouaji* had taken. At the same time he felt softly of his wallet in his breast pocket. Then he spat over the edge of the cliff. Then he made water over it, and listened intently, like a child. This gave him the impetus to start down the path into the abyss. Curiously enough, he was not dizzy. But prudently he kept from peering to his right, over the edge. It was a steady and steep downward climb. The monotony of it put him into a frame of mind not unlike that which had been induced by the bus ride. He was murmuring 'Hassan Ramani' again, repeatedly and in rhythm. He stopped, furious with himself for the sinister overtones the name now suggested to him. He decided he was exhausted from the trip. 'And the walk,' he added.

He was now well down the gigantic cliff, but the moon, being directly overhead, gave as much light as ever. Only the wind was left behind, above, to wander among the trees, to blow through the dusty streets of Aïn Tadouirt, into the hall of the Grand Hotel Saharien, and under the door of his little room.

It occurred to him that he ought to ask himself why he was doing this irrational thing, but he was intelligent enough to know that since he was doing it, it was not so important to probe for explanations at that moment.

Suddenly the earth was flat beneath his feet. He had reached the bottom sooner than he had expected. He stepped ahead distrustfully still, as if he expected another treacherous drop. It was so hard to know in this uniform, dim brightness. Before he knew what had happened the dog was upon him, a heavy mass of fur trying to push him backwards, a sharp nail rubbing down his chest, a straining of muscles against him to get the teeth into his neck. The Professor thought: I refuse to die this way. The dog fell back; it looked like an Eskimo dog. As it sprang again, he called out, very loud: 'Ay!' It fell against him, there was a confusion of sensations and a pain somewhere. There was also the sound of voices very near to him, and he could not understand what they were saying. Something cold and metallic was pushed brutally against his spine as the dog still hung for a second by his teeth from a mass of clothing and perhaps flesh. The Professor knew it was a gun, and he raised his hands, shouting in Moghrebi: 'Take away the dog!' But the gun merely pushed him forward, and since the dog, once it was back on the ground, did not leap again, he took a step ahead. The gun kept pushing; he kept taking steps. Again he heard voices, but the person directly behind him said nothing. People seemed to be running about; it sounded that way, at least. For his eyes, he discovered, were still shut tight against the dog's attack. He opened them. A group of men was advancing toward him. They were dressed in the black clothes of the Reguibat. 'The Reguiba is a cloud across the face of the sun.' 'When the Reguiba appears the righteous man turns away.' In how many shops and market-places he had heard these maxims uttered banteringly among friends.

Never to a Reguiba, to be sure, for these men do not frequent towns. They send a representative in disguise, to arrange with shady elements there for the disposal of captured goods. An opportunity, he thought quickly, of testing the accuracy of such statements. He did not doubt for a moment that the adventure would prove to be a kind of warning against such foolishness on his part – a warning which in retrospect would be half sinister, half farcical.

Two snarling dogs came running from behind the oncoming men and threw themselves at his legs. He was scandalized to note that no one paid any attention to this breach of etiquette. The gun pushed him harder as he tried to sidestep the animals' noisy assault. Again he cried: 'The dogs! Take them away!' The gun shoved him forward with great force and he fell, almost at the feet of the crowd of men facing him. The dogs were wrenching at his hands and arms. A boot kicked them aside, yelping, and then with increased vigour it kicked the Professor in the hip. Then came a chorus of kicks from different sides, and he was rolled violently about on the earth for a while. During this time he was conscious of hands reaching into his pockets and removing everything from them. He tried to say: 'You have all my money; stop kicking me!' But his bruised facial muscles would not work; he felt himself pouting, and that was all. Someone dealt him a terrific blow on the head, and he thought: Now at least I shall lose consciousness, thank heaven. Still he went on being aware of the guttural voices he could not understand, and of being bound tightly about the ankles and chest. Then there was black silence that opened like a wound from time to time, to let in the soft, deep notes of the flute playing the same succession of notes again and again. Suddenly he felt excruciating pain everywhere – pain and cold. So I have been unconscious, after all, he thought. In spite of that, the present seemed only like a direct continuation of what had gone before.

It was growing faintly light. There were camels near where he was lying; he could hear their gurgling and their heavy breathing. He could not bring himself to attempt opening his eyes, just in case it should turn out to be impossible. However, when he heard someone approaching, he found that he had no difficulty in seeing.

The man looked at him dispassionately in the grey morning light. With one hand he pinched together the Professor's nostrils. When the Professor opened his mouth to breathe, the man swiftly seized his tongue and pulled on it with all his might. The Professor was gagging and catching his breath; he did not see what was happening. He could not distinguish the pain of the brutal yanking from that of the sharp knife. Then there was an endless choking and spitting that went on automatically, as though he were scarcely a part of it. The word 'operation' kept going through his mind; it calmed his terror somewhat as he sank back into darkness.

The caravan left sometime toward mid-morning. The Professor, not unconscious, but in a state of utter stupor, still gagging and drooling blood, was dumped doubled up into a sack and tied at one side of a camel. The lower end of the enormous amphitheatre contained a natural gate in the rocks. The camels, swift *mehara*, were lightly laden on this trip. They passed through single file, and slowly mounted the gentle slope that led up into the beginning of the desert. That night, at a stop behind some low hills, the men took him out, still in a state which permitted no thought, and over the dusty rags that remained of his clothing they fastened a series of curious belts made of the bottoms of tin cans strung together. One after another of these bright girdles was wired about his torso, his arms and legs, even across his face, until he was entirely within a suit of armour that covered him with its circular metal scales. There was a good deal of merriment during this decking-out of the Professor. One man brought out a flute and a younger one did a not ungraceful caricature of an Ouled Naïl executing a cane dance. The Professor was no longer conscious; to be exact, he existed in the middle of the movements made by these other men. When they had finished dressing him the way they wished him to look, they stuffed some food under the tin bangles hanging over his face. Even though he chewed mechanically, most of it eventually fell out on to the ground. They put him back into the sack and left him there.

Two days later they arrived at one of their own encampments. There were women and children here in the tents, and the men had to drive away the snarling dogs they had left there to guard them. When they emptied the Professor out of his sack, there were screams of fright, and it took several hours to convince the last woman that he was harmless, although there had been no doubt from the start that he was a valuable possession. After a few days they began to move on again, taking everything with them, and travelling only at night as the terrain grew warmer.

Even when all his wounds had healed and he felt no more pain, the Professor did not begin to think again; he ate and defecated, and he danced when he was bidden, a senseless hopping up and down that delighted the children, principally because of the wonderful jangling racket it made. And he generally slept through the heat of the day, in among the camels.

Wending its way south-east, the caravan avoided all stationary civilization. In a few weeks they reached a new plateau, wholly wild and with a sparse vegetation. Here they pitched camp and remained, while the *mehara* were turned loose to graze. Everyone was happy here; the weather was cooler and there was a well only a few hours away on a seldom frequented trail. It was here they conceived the idea of taking the Professor to Fogara and selling him to the Touareg.

It was a full year before they carried out this project. By this time the Professor was much better trained. He could do a handspring, make a series of fearful growling noises which had, nevertheless, a certain element of humour; and when the Reguibat removed the tin from his face they discovered he could grimace admirably while he danced. They also taught him a few basic obscene gestures which never failed to elicit delighted shrieks from the women. He was now brought forth only after especially abundant meals, when there was music and festivity. He easily fell in with their sense of ritual, and evolved an elementary sort of 'programme' to present when he was called for: dancing, rolling on the ground, imitating certain animals, and finally rushing toward the group in feigned anger, to see the resultant confusion and hilarity.

When three of the men set out for Fogara with him, they

took four *mehara* with them, and he rode astride his quite naturally. No precautions were taken to guard him, save that he was kept among them, one man always staying at the rear of the party. They came within sight of the walls at dawn, and they waited among the rocks all day. At dusk the youngest started out, and in three hours he returned with a friend who carried a stout cane. They tried to put the Professor through his routine then and there, but the man from Fogara was in a hurry to get back to town, so they all set out on the *mehara*.

In the town they went directly to the villager's home, where they had coffee in the courtyard sitting among the camels. Here the Professor went into his act again, and this time there was prolonged merriment and much rubbing together of hands. An agreement was reached, a sum of money paid, and the Reguibat withdrew, leaving the Professor in the house of the man with the cane, who did not delay in locking him into a tiny enclosure off the courtyard.

The next day was an important one in the Professor's life, for it was then that pain began to stir again in his being. A group of men came to the house, among whom was a venerable gentleman, better clothed than those others who spent their time flattering him, setting fervent kisses upon his hands and the edges of his garments. This person made a point of going into classical Arabic from time to time, to impress the others, who had not learned a word of the Koran. Thus his conversation would run more or less as follows: 'Perhaps at In Salah. The French there are stupid. Celestial vengeance is approaching. Let us not hasten it. Praise the highest and cast thine anathema against idols. With paint on his face. In case the police wish to look close.' The others listened and agreed, nodding their heads slowly and solemnly. And the Professor in his stall beside them listened, too. That is, he was *conscious* of the sound of the old man's Arabic. The words penetrated for the first time in many months. Noises, then: 'Celestial vengeance is approaching.' Then: 'It is an honour. Fifty francs is enough. Keep your money. Good.' And the *qaouaji* squatting near him at the edge of the precipice. Then 'anathema against idols' and more gibberish. He turned over panting on the sand and forgot about it. But the pain had begun. It operated in a kind of delirium, because he had begun to enter into consciousness again. When the man opened the door and prodded him with his cane, he cried out in a rage, and everyone laughed.

They got him on to his feet, but he would not dance. He stood before them, staring at the ground, stubbornly refusing to move. The owner was furious, and so annoyed by the laughter of the others that he felt obliged to send them away, saying that he would await a more propitious time for exhibiting his property, because he dared not show his anger before the elder. However, when they had left he dealt the Professor a violent blow on the shoulder with his cane, called him various obscene things, and went out into the street, slamming the gate behind him. He walked straight to the street of the Ouled Naïl, because he was sure of finding the Reguibat there among the girls, spending the money. And there in a tent he found one of them still abed, while an Ouled Naïl washed the tea glasses. He walked in and almost decapitated the man before the latter had even attempted to sit up. Then he threw his razor on the bed and ran out.

The Ouled Naïl saw the blood, screamed, ran out of her tent into the next, and soon emerged from that with four girls who rushed together into the coffee house and told the *qaouaji* who had killed the Reguiba. It was only a matter of an hour before the French military police had caught him at a friend's house, and dragged him off to the barracks. That night the Professor had nothing to eat, and the next afternoon, in the slow sharpening of his consciousness caused by increasing hunger, he walked aimlessly about the court-yard and the rooms that gave on to it. There was no one. In one room a calendar hung on the wall. The Professor watched nervously, like a dog watching a fly in front of its nose. On the white paper were black objects that made sounds in his head. He heard them: '*Grande Epicerie du Sahel. Juin. Lundi, mardi, mercredi....*'

The tiny ink-marks of which a symphony consists may have been made long ago, but when they are fulfilled in sound they become imminent and mighty. So a kind of music of feeling began to play in the Professor's head, increasing in volume as he looked at the mud wall, and he had the feeling that he was performing what had been written for him long ago. He felt like weeping; he felt like roaring through the little house, upsetting and smashing the few breakable objects. His emotion got no further than this one overwhelming desire. So, bellowing as loud as he could, he attacked the house and its belongings. Then he attacked the door into the street, which resisted for a while and finally broke. He climbed through the opening made by the boards he had ripped apart, and still bellowing and shaking his arms in the air to make as loud a jangling as possible, he began to gallop along the quiet street toward the gateway of the town. A few people looked at him with great curiosity. As he passed the garage, the last building before the high mud archway that framed the desert beyond, a French soldier saw him. *Tiens*, he said to himself, a holy maniac.

Again it was sunset time. The Professor ran beneath the arched gate, turned his face toward the red sky, and began to trot along the Piste d'In Salah, straight into the setting sun. Behind him, from the garage, the soldier took a pot shot at him for good luck. The bullet whistled dangerously near the Professor's head, and his yelling rose into an indignant lament as he waved his arms more wildly, and hopped high into the air at every few steps, in an access of terror.

The soldier watched a while, smiling, as the cavorting figure grew smaller in the oncoming evening darkness, and the rattling of the tin became a part of the great silence out there beyond the gate. The wall of the garage as he leaned against it still gave forth heat, left there by the sun, but even then the lunar chill was growing in the air.